The Last Breath

Shane Reed

Copyright

Chapter 1

Billy wiped his calloused hands on his faded jeans, a habitual gesture that left grease stains on the denim. Another shift done. Another day wasted. He glanced at the clock - 5:30 PM. Right on schedule.

"See you tomorrow, Billy," called Marge from the front desk.

"Yeah, see ya," he replied with a practiced smile that didn't reach his eyes.

Billy pushed through the heavy metal doors of the community center. The late afternoon sun hit him like a spotlight, long shadows stretching across cracked pavement. He squinted, adjusting his worn baseball cap.

Stepping onto the sidewalk, Billy let out a weary sigh. Home. What a joke. Just another dingy apartment in an endless string of temporary residences.

He started walking, mind already racing. How much was left in his wallet? Enough for rent? Food? The numbers never added up.

A memory flashed - polishing silverware in Mrs. Henderson's room at Sunny Pines Retirement Village. All those valuables, just sitting there. Unguarded. Wasted on people with one foot in the grave.

Billy shook his head, banishing the thought. For now.

The shadows grew longer as he trudged on. Another day down. How many more could he take?

Billy's footsteps echoed hollowly on the cracked sidewalk as he made his way through the quiet streets. The fading sunlight cast a sickly yellow glow on the peeling paint of the houses lining the road, their dilapidated state a mirror to his own weary soul.

"Damn, this place is falling apart," he muttered, kicking a loose piece of concrete. "Just like me."

His eyes darted from house to house, cataloging details with the precision of a predator. Rusty car in the driveway. Overgrown lawn. Curtains drawn tight. All signs of struggle, of lives barely held together.

Billy's mind raced, calculating furiously. "Two hundred in the bank. Maybe fifty in cash. Rent's due in a week. Fuck."

He passed the local diner, its neon sign flickering weakly. The smell of grease and desperation wafted out, making his stomach turn.

"Could pick up an extra shift," he mused, then immediately rejected the idea. "Nah, waste of time. Gotta think bigger."

A police siren wailed in the distance, setting Billy's nerves on edge. He quickened his pace, hands shoved deep in his pockets.

"Keep it cool, Billy boy," he whispered to himself. "You're just another nobody in this shit town. For now."

The frustration bubbled beneath his calm exterior, a volcano ready to erupt. He needed a plan, and fast. The mundane couldn't hold him much longer. Something had to give.

As Billy trudged along, his mind drifted back to his stint at Sunnyvale Retirement Home. The memory was vivid, almost tactile.

"Good morning, Mrs. Hawkins," he heard himself say, his voice dripping with manufactured warmth. "Let's get you ready for breakfast."

Billy's eyes scanned the room, noting the ornate jewelry box on the dresser, the gleaming silver picture frames. His gaze lingered on a sparkling diamond ring left carelessly on the nightstand.

"Such pretty things," he murmured, helping the frail woman into her wheelchair. "Must be worth a fortune."

Mrs. Hawkins patted his hand, her rheumy eyes filled with trust. "You're such a dear, Billy."

He smiled, but his mind raced with calculations. How easy it would be to slip that ring into his pocket. Who would notice? Who would care?

The memory faded as Billy reached his apartment building. The concrete steps were cracked, weeds pushing through like stubborn reminders of neglect. He grasped the rusted railing, feeling it wobble under his weight.

"Home sweet home," he muttered, fishing for his keys.

The door creaked ominously as he pushed it open, the sound echoing in the empty hallway. Billy paused, listening for any signs of life. Nothing but the hum of flickering fluorescent lights greeted him.

"Perfect," he whispered, a plan already forming in his mind. "Time to make a change."

Billy stumbled into his apartment, tossing his keys onto the cluttered table by the door. They skittered across its surface, coming to rest against a stack of unpaid bills. His eyes swept the room, taking in the bare walls and threadbare furniture.

"Home, crappy home," he muttered, kicking off his shoes.

The sparse furnishings seemed to mock him. A sagging couch, a rickety coffee table, and a small TV on a wobbly stand. It was a far cry from the opulent rooms he'd glimpsed in his various jobs.

Billy's hand instinctively reached for his back pocket, pulling out his worn wallet. He flipped it open, his fingers trembling slightly as he counted the meager contents.

"Twenty... forty... sixty... eighty-five," he whispered, his jaw clenching. "Pathetic."

He slumped onto the couch, the springs groaning in protest. His mind raced, calculating bills, rent, groceries. The numbers didn't add up, no matter how he twisted them.

"This can't go on," Billy muttered, staring at the cracked ceiling. "I'm better than this. Smarter than this."

His fingers drummed against the arm of the couch, a rhythmic counterpoint to his racing thoughts. The faces of elderly residents flashed through his mind, their trusting smiles, their unguarded possessions.

"They have so much," he reasoned, his voice barely above a whisper. "Would they even notice if...?"

Billy sat up straight, a new resolve hardening his features. He glanced around the dingy apartment, his decision crystallizing.

"No more Mr. Nice Guy," he declared to the empty room. "It's time to take what I deserve."

The memory washed over Billy, vivid and sharp. He was back in the Sunnyside Retirement Community, crouched under a sink, wrench in hand.

"Almost got it, Mrs. Hawkins," he called out, his voice cheerful and reassuring.

The faucet gave a final stubborn sputter before surrendering to his efforts. As he emerged, wiping his hands on a rag, his eyes darted around the lavishly decorated room.

"Oh, thank you, dear," Mrs. Hawkins beamed, her gnarled hands clutching a delicate porcelain figurine. "You're such a blessing."

Billy's gaze lingered on the figurine, then swept across the room, cataloging. Antique silver frames. A Tiffany lamp. Jewelry boxes barely concealing glittering treasures.

"Just doing my job, ma'am," he replied, flashing a disarming smile. "Happy to help."

As he packed up his tools, his mind raced. How easy it would be to slip that figurine into his bag. Who would suspect the friendly maintenance man?

The memory faded, and Billy found himself back on his threadbare couch, staring at the water-stained ceiling. His fingers absently traced the worn fabric beneath him.

"I could've had it all," he muttered, bitterness seeping into his voice. "Instead, I'm stuck in this dump, living paycheck to paycheck."

He sat up abruptly, running a hand through his disheveled hair. "All those opportunities, right there for the taking. And I was too damn scared to grab them."

Billy's eyes narrowed, a newfound determination hardening his features. "Not anymore," he declared to the empty room. "It's time to stop playing by the rules. Time to take what's mine."

Billy's leg bounced restlessly as he leaned forward, elbows on knees, hands clasped tight. His gaze darted around the dingy apartment, landing on a framed photo of Sunny Meadows Retirement Community.

"Those old folks," he muttered, a twisted smile playing at his lips. "So trusting. So... vulnerable."

He stood abruptly, pacing the small space. "It'd be easy. In and out. They probably wouldn't even notice."

Billy paused, catching his reflection in a cracked mirror. "What's stopping you?" he asked his image. "You've always been good at blending in, being the nice guy everyone trusts."

His hands clenched into fists. "No more Mr. Nice Guy. It's time to cash in on all that goodwill."

With sudden purpose, Billy strode to a cluttered desk, rifling through papers. "I still have those floor plans from when I worked maintenance," he murmured, triumph in his voice.

He turned, surveying the shabby room with new eyes. "This ends now," Billy declared, resolve hardening his features. "No more scraping by. No more settling."

His gaze landed on his worn baseball cap. He snatched it up, jamming it on his head. "Time to create my own opportunities," Billy said, a cold glint in his eye. "And Sunny Meadows is just the beginning."

Chapter 2

Billy's knuckles rapped against the weathered oak door. Three sharp knocks. He adjusted his worn baseball cap, a practiced smile sliding into place. Showtime.

The door creaked open, revealing Mrs. Johnson's vibrant face. Her red curls bounced as she beamed at him.

"Oh, Billy! Right on time. Come in, come in!"

He stepped inside, his eyes darting around the entryway. Old photos. Antique vase. Nothing worthwhile yet.

"How are you today, Mrs. Johnson?" Billy's voice oozed warmth, masking the cold calculation beneath.

"Just lovely, dear. And please, call me Lou. Mrs. Johnson makes me feel ancient!"

She laughed, a sound that grated on Billy's nerves. He forced a chuckle.

"Right this way," Lou chirped, leading him towards the kitchen. "That faucet's been driving me batty."

Billy's gaze swept the living room as they passed. Trinkets everywhere. But what was actually valuable?

"Here we are," Lou announced, gesturing to the sink.

Billy nodded, setting down his toolbox. "No worries, Lou. I'll have this fixed up in no time."

His eyes locked onto a small safe tucked in the corner. Jackpot.

"Is there anything else you need while I'm here?" Billy asked, his mind already plotting.

Lou tapped her chin. "Well, now that you mention it..."

Billy tensed. What else could she reveal?

Billy knelt by the sink, tools in hand, his mind racing. What other secrets might this old woman's house hold?

"You know, Billy," Lou began, settling onto a nearby stool, "this kitchen reminds me so much of my Frank."

Billy grunted noncommittally, focusing on the pipes. Keep her talking, he thought.

"Oh, the adventures we had!" Lou's eyes sparkled. "Did I ever tell you about the time we backpacked through Peru?"

"Can't say you have," Billy replied, his tone carefully interested. What's the point of this story?

Lou launched into a tale of mountain treks and ancient ruins. Billy half-listened, his fingers working methodically on the faucet. His eyes, however, kept darting to the safe in the corner.

"...and that's when Frank pulled out his grandfather's watch," Lou continued, her voice softening. "Said it got him through the war, and now it'd get us through the Andes."

Billy's ears perked up. A war relic? Those could fetch a pretty penny.

"Sounds like quite a timepiece," he remarked, feigning casual interest.

Lou nodded enthusiastically. "Oh, it is! A real beauty. I keep it in my jewelry box now, can't bear to part with it."

Billy's heart raced. Bingo. "That's really something," he said, his mind already calculating potential profits. "Must be worth a fortune."

"I suppose it is," Lou mused. "But the memories are priceless."

Billy tightened the last bolt, his plan crystallizing. He'd be back for that watch, and soon.

Billy wiped his hands on a rag, straightening up from the sink. "All done, Mrs. Johnson. That should take care of the leak."

"Oh, wonderful!" Lou exclaimed, her face lighting up with that infectious smile. "You're a lifesaver, Billy. How can I ever thank you?"

He shrugged, feigning modesty. "Just doing my job, ma'am. No need for thanks."

As Lou led him towards the front door, Billy's eyes darted around, mapping the layout. There, on the dresser in the hallway is an ornate wooden box. That had to be it.

"You know," Lou said, pausing by the door, "you remind me a bit of Frank when he was younger. Always so helpful."

Billy forced a smile, his hand on the doorknob. "That's kind of you to say, Mrs. Johnson. Take care now."

As he stepped out onto the porch, Lou called after him, "Do come by for tea sometime, dear!"

"Sure thing," Billy replied, not turning back. His mind was already racing, possibilities unfurling before him like a road map.

Walking to his van, Billy's thoughts churned. It would be so easy. One quick break-in, grab the watch, and he'd be set for months. He deserved this, didn't he? After all those years of scraping by, living paycheck to paycheck while others had it easy.

"It's not fair," he muttered, slamming the van door shut. "I've worked hard. What's one little score compared to a lifetime of getting the short end of the stick?"

As he drove away, Billy's resolve hardened. He'd make things right, balance the scales. And Mrs. Johnson? She'd barely miss one watch among her treasures. It was practically a victimless crime.

Billy's fingers flew across the keyboard, his eyes glued to the screen. The glow of the monitor cast harsh shadows across his face in the dimly lit apartment.

"Bingo," he muttered, jotting down an address. "Vintage Treasures. Specializes in antique watches."

He opened another tab, searching for more pawn shops. The list grew longer, each one a potential goldmine.

Billy leaned back, rubbing his eyes. "Gotta be smart about this. Can't hit the same place twice."

His phone buzzed. A notification from an online forum. Billy tapped it, eyes widening as he scrolled.

"Holy shit," he whispered. "A Patek Philippe from the 1920s? That's gotta be worth a fortune."

He dove deeper into the forum, absorbing every detail about valuable heirlooms. The more he read, the more his excitement grew.

"It's not like Lou needs all that stuff," Billy reasoned aloud. "She's had her time. Her adventures. What about me?"

He stood up, pacing the small room. "I'm just evening the score. Taking what should've been mine all along."

Billy's mind raced with possibilities. The watch. The jewelry box. Who knew what other treasures Lou had stashed away?

"It's not stealing," he told himself. "It's... redistribution. Yeah, that's it. I'm Robin Hood, taking from the rich and giving to the poor. Me."

He laughed, a sharp, humorless sound. "About time someone looked out for Billy Thompson."

Billy glanced at the clock on his microwave. 9:37 PM. He drummed his fingers on the kitchen counter, mind racing.

"Lou's probably winding down for the night," he muttered. "Early to bed, early to rise. That's how these old folks operate."

He pictured Mrs. Johnson's daily routine, piecing together snippets from their conversations. "She mentioned her book club meets on Thursdays. That's my window."

Billy grabbed a notepad, scribbling furiously. "Enter through the back. Maintenance check on the water heater. Perfect excuse."

He paused, tapping the pen against his chin. "But what if she's not home? Need a backup plan."

"Hey, Mrs. J!" Billy practiced, his voice shifting to a cheerful, concerned tone. "Just swinging by to make sure everything's okay with that faucet. Mind if I take a quick look?"

He grinned, satisfied with his performance. "She'll eat it up. Trusting old bat."

Billy's eyes darted to the toolbox by the door. "Gotta look the part. Screwdriver... wrench... perfect for jimmying open that jewelry box if needed."

He grabbed the tools, weighing them in his hands. "Quick in, quick out. Five minutes tops."

"And if she catches me?" Billy muttered, a flicker of doubt crossing his face. He shook it off. "Nah, she won't. I'm too smart for that."

He rehearsed his lines again, fine-tuning his approach. Each repetition bolstered his confidence.

"This is it, Billy boy," he said to himself. "Your ticket out of this dump. No more scraping by. No more kowtowing to entitled geezers."

Billy's eyes gleamed with anticipation. "Time to take what's rightfully mine."

Billy leaned closer to the bathroom mirror, his face illuminated by the harsh fluorescent light. His reflection stared back, but something was different. The usual friendly maintenance worker façade had slipped away, revealing a cold, calculating gaze.

"Well, well," he murmured, a smirk tugging at the corner of his mouth. "Who's this handsome devil?"

He ran a hand through his unkempt brown hair, studying the transformation. The baseball cap was off, exposing a man who looked sharper, more focused. Dangerous.

"You've been hiding, haven't you?" Billy whispered to his reflection. "All those years of playing nice, blending in. But not anymore."

He straightened up, shoulders back, chin lifted. The change was subtle but unmistakable. A predator emerging from its camouflage.

"Mrs. Johnson won't know what hit her," he chuckled darkly. "Poor thing probably thinks I'm her friend. If only she knew."

Billy's mind raced with anticipation. He felt a surge of power coursing through him, electrifying every nerve.

"This is who I was meant to be," he said, his voice low and intense. "No more scraps. No more second-hand life. I'm taking what I deserve."

He leaned in closer, his breath fogging the mirror. "You hear that, world? Billy Thompson is done playing by your rules. It's my turn now."

With a final nod to his reflection, Billy's lips curled into a sinister grin. "Show time."

Billy's hand hovered over the light switch, his eyes locked on his shadowy reflection. The bathroom suddenly felt too small, constricting.

"Time to step out of the shadows," he muttered, flicking off the light.

Darkness enveloped him, but Billy's vision had never been clearer. He navigated through his cramped apartment with newfound purpose, each step deliberate.

In the living room, he paused by the window. Streetlights cast an eerie glow on the empty sidewalk below. Perfect conditions for what lay ahead.

"Just like any other job," Billy reminded himself, his voice steady. "In and out. Clean and simple."

He grabbed his toolbox—a prop that had served him well countless times before. Its weight felt different now, heavier with intent.

As he reached for the door, a fleeting image of Mrs. Johnson's kind face flashed in his mind. Billy shook it off, jaw clenching.

"Can't afford sentimentality," he growled. "She's just another mark. Nothing personal."

He opened the door, the cool night air rushing in. Billy took a deep breath, savoring the moment.

"Game on, Mrs. Johnson," he whispered into the darkness. "Let's see what that family heirloom of yours is really worth."

With that, Billy stepped out, leaving behind the last traces of his former self. The path ahead was clear, and nothing would stand in his way.

Chapter 3

Billy tugged at the collar of his faded blue uniform, adjusting the cap that shadowed his eyes. Sunset Meadows loomed before him, its manicured lawns and cheerful flower beds a stark contrast to the darkness coiled within him.

His gaze swept the grounds, cataloging every detail. An old man shuffled along with a walker. A sprinkler ticked rhythmically nearby. The air hung heavy with the scent of freshly cut grass.

Perfect. Quiet. Unsuspecting.

Billy's lips curved into a practiced smile as he hefted his toolbox. Just another maintenance man, nothing to see here. The weight of the tools inside - screwdrivers, wrenches, pliers - felt comforting. Familiar. Like old friends.

He set off toward Martha Simmons' apartment, footsteps measured and unhurried. No need to rush. No need to draw attention.

"Morning!" he called, waving to a pair of elderly women on a bench. They smiled and waved back, already dismissing him from their minds.

That's right. Look right past me. I'm nobody important.

The thrill of deception sent a shiver down his spine. They had no idea what he was capable of. What he was about to do.

Billy approached Martha's door, heart quickening despite his outward calm. One more job. One more score. Then he could disappear, start fresh somewhere new. Somewhere no one would ever suspect the mild-mannered handyman of such heinous acts.

He raised his hand to knock, allowing himself a final moment to savor the anticipation. The hunt. The thrill.

Time to go to work.

Billy rapped his knuckles against the door, three sharp taps. "Maintenance!" he called out, his voice warm and friendly. "Just here to check on that leaky faucet, ma'am."

The door creaked open, revealing Martha Simmons' weathered face. Her eyes, still sharp despite her age, scanned Billy from head to toe.

"I don't remember reporting any leak," she said, her brow furrowing.

Billy's smile never wavered. "Oh, it was actually your neighbor, Mrs. Johnson. She mentioned hearing water running from your unit." He tapped his temple. "Better safe than sorry, right?"

Martha's eyes narrowed, studying Billy's face intently. He could almost see the gears turning in her mind, weighing his words against her suspicion.

Is she buying it? Billy's heart raced, but his expression remained placid. Just another day on the job.

"Well, I suppose it wouldn't hurt to check," Martha finally relented, her shoulders relaxing slightly. She stepped back, opening the door wider. "Come on in, young man."

"Thank you, ma'am," Billy said, tipping his cap as he entered. "I'll be quick, promise. Don't want to disturb your morning any more than necessary."

As he crossed the threshold, Billy's keen eyes darted around, taking in every detail of Martha's apartment. The layout, the furnishings, potential exit routes—all filed away in his mental catalogue.

Just another job, he reminded himself, tamping down the surge of adrenaline. In and out, nice and easy.

Billy's eyes swept the room, cataloging every detail. A gleaming mahogany cabinet caught his attention. Antique, probably valuable. His gaze flickered to a display case filled with delicate porcelain figurines. Easy to pocket, easier to sell.

"The kitchen's this way," Martha said, shuffling towards a narrow hallway.

Billy followed, his movements fluid and unhurried. "Appreciate it, ma'am. Won't take but a moment."

As they entered the kitchen, Billy's mind raced. Now or never. He glanced at Martha's frail form. One quick move...

"Actually," he said, his voice suddenly tight, "I think I left a tool in my truck. Mind if I grab it real quick?"

Martha turned, confusion etched on her face. "I suppose—"

Billy lunged, his hand clamping over her mouth. She struggled, eyes wide with terror, but he was already forcing her down. His other hand found a decorative pillow on a nearby chair.

This is it, he thought, a cold calm settling over him. Just like we practiced.

Martha's muffled screams were cut short as he pressed the pillow over her face. Her arms flailed, nails raking his skin, but Billy held firm.

"Shh," he whispered, almost tenderly. "It'll be over soon."

The struggle was brief, intense. Billy's muscles strained as he maintained pressure, watching dispassionately as Martha's movements grew weaker.

It's necessary, he told himself. A means to an end. Nothing personal.

As Martha's body went limp, a mix of exhilaration and nausea washed over Billy. He checked her pulse, ensuring the deed was done.

Now for the real work, he thought, straightening up and smoothing his uniform. Time to make this look natural.

Billy's eyes darted around the room, assessing. "Where's the good stuff, Martha?" he muttered, his voice a low rasp.

He moved swiftly to the bedroom, yanking open drawers. His fingers, steady despite the adrenaline, sifted through clothing. Nothing.

"Come on, come on," he hissed.

A glint caught his eye. The jewelry box. Ornate, antique. Billy's lips curled into a smile.

"Jackpot."

He flipped the lid, revealing a treasure trove. Pearls, diamonds, gold. Each piece disappeared into his pockets with practiced efficiency.

A voice in his head urged caution. Don't get greedy. Take what you can fence easily.

Billy paused, weighing a emerald necklace. "Sorry, sweetheart," he whispered. "Can't risk it."

He returned to Martha's body, his movements precise. Gently, he lifted her, arranging her on the bed. He smoothed her hair, adjusted her nightgown.

Just sleeping, he thought. Nothing more.

Billy stepped back, scrutinizing his work. "Sweet dreams, Martha," he murmured, a hint of genuine remorse coloring his tone.

No loose ends, he reminded himself. Make it look natural.

He placed a half-empty glass of water on the nightstand, positioned an open book face-down beside it.

Perfect, Billy thought. Just another quiet night at Sunset Meadows.

Billy's hand hesitated on the doorknob, his breath catching as he heard footsteps approaching in the hallway. He squared his shoulders, adopting an easy smile as he stepped out.

"Evening," a cheerful voice greeted him. Mrs. Donovan, 82, arthritis-bent but sharp-eyed, shuffled past with her walker.

"Good evening, ma'am," Billy replied, tipping his cap. His voice was warm, practiced. "Just finished up some maintenance for Mrs. Simmons. Everything's ship-shape now."

Mrs. Donovan beamed. "Oh, how lovely. You're such a dear, always helping us old folks."

Billy chuckled, the sound hollow in his ears. "It's my pleasure. You folks deserve the best."

"Well, don't work too hard, young man," she said, patting his arm.

"I won't. You have a good night now," Billy responded, his heart thundering beneath his calm exterior.

As Mrs. Donovan continued down the hall, Billy exhaled slowly. He strode towards the exit, his pace measured, unhurried. Just another day at work, he reminded himself.

Pushing through the lobby doors, the cool night air hit his face. Billy paused, scanning the parking lot. Empty. Silent. Perfect.

He allowed himself a small smile. You've done it again, Thompson, he thought. Clean getaway.

Billy's footsteps crunched on the gravel as he walked towards his car, adrenaline surging through his veins. His mind raced, reliving the past hour in vivid flashes.

"Too easy," he muttered, a mix of pride and unease coloring his thoughts. "They're all so trusting, so... vulnerable." He flexed his fingers, still feeling the resistance of the pillow against Martha's face.

The thrill of success battled with a nagging fear. What if he'd missed something? Left a trace?

"No," Billy reassured himself. "You were careful. Methodical. Just like always."

He reached his nondescript sedan, parked far from the building's security cameras. As he popped the trunk, a grin spread across his face.

"One down," he whispered, placing the toolbox inside. "Who's next on the list?"

Billy's mind whirred with possibilities. "Maybe that widower on the third floor? Or the retired judge?" He chuckled softly. "So many options, so little time."

Slamming the trunk shut, he paused, savoring the moment. The cool metal of the car against his palm grounded him, reminding him of his success.

"You've still got it, Billy boy," he murmured, sliding into the driver's seat. "They'll never see you coming."

With a final glance at Sunset Meadows in his rearview mirror, Billy started the engine. The purr of the car matched the thrum of excitement in his veins as he pulled away, already plotting his next move.

As Billy's car disappeared around the corner, Sunset Meadows settled back into its deceptive tranquility. The late afternoon sun cast long shadows across the manicured lawns, painting the scene in warm hues of orange and gold. A gentle breeze rustled through the carefully trimmed hedges, carrying the faint scent of blooming roses.

On the surface, nothing seemed amiss. Residents shuffled along the winding paths, some with walkers, others arm-in-arm with visiting family members. Laughter drifted from the community center, where a spirited game of bingo was underway.

But behind the idyllic facade, a darkness now lurked.

In Martha Simmons' apartment, the silence was oppressive. The ticking of her antique clock on the mantle seemed to echo unnaturally loud, counting down the minutes until her body would be discovered.

Outside her window, a hummingbird hovered near a feeder, its wings a blur of motion. It paused, as if sensing something amiss, before darting away.

A maintenance worker - a real one this time - whistled as he pushed his cart down the hallway, oblivious to the horror that lay just behind one of the doors he passed.

At the front desk, the receptionist greeted new visitors with a warm smile, unaware that she had inadvertently allowed a predator into their midst.

As dusk began to fall, the soft glow of lights from countless windows created a patchwork of warmth against the deepening sky. From a distance, Sunset Meadows looked like a haven of peace and security.

But within its walls, a killer's handiwork lay hidden, waiting to shatter the illusion of safety that its residents held so dear.

Chapter 4

The bell's soft jingle echoed through the musty air as Billy stepped into the dimly lit pawn shop. His eyes, sharp beneath the brim of his stained baseball cap, scanned the glass cases lining the walls. Trinkets and treasures glimmered dully in the weak light.

Billy's fingers twitched, ghosting over the velvet pouch in his pocket. Martha's jewelry. His latest score. He approached the counter with measured steps, careful to keep his face neutral.

"Afternoon," he said, mimicking the casual drawl of the locals. "Got something you might be interested in."

The pawnbroker looked up, his weathered face creasing with interest. "Let's see what you've got, son."

Billy's heart quickened as he placed the pouch on the counter. Just another transaction, he reminded himself. Nothing to arouse suspicion.

The broker's gnarled hands deftly untied the pouch, spilling its contents onto the glass surface. Diamonds winked in the fluorescent light. Gold chains coiled like snakes.

"Nice pieces," the broker murmured, lifting a necklace to examine it closely.

Billy watched, tension coiling in his gut. Would the old man recognize the jewelry? Ask questions?

"Family heirloom," Billy offered, the lie slipping easily from his tongue. "Hard times, you know how it is."

The broker grunted, noncommittal. His magnifying glass came out, hovering over each piece in turn.

Billy's palms grew damp. He resisted the urge to wipe them on his jeans. Stay calm, he coached himself. You've done this before. You're just another down-on-his-luck guy pawning some jewelry.

"I can give you eight hundred for the lot," the broker said finally, looking up.

Billy's pulse jumped. More than he'd expected. "Sounds fair," he replied, careful to keep the eagerness from his voice.

As the broker counted out crisp bills, Billy's mind raced. This score would keep him comfortable for a while. But the thrill, the hunger for more, already gnawed at him. Who would be next? Another lonely old woman, ripe for the picking?

The cash changed hands. Billy pocketed it, savoring the weight. A tangible reward for his cunning, his nerve. The adrenaline of the score still hummed in his veins.

"Pleasure doing business," he said, tipping his cap to the broker.

As he turned to leave, Billy allowed himself a small, satisfied smile. They never saw him coming. And they never would.

The bell jingled as Billy pushed through the pawn shop door, stepping out into the fading afternoon light. His fingers traced the outline of the cash in his pocket, a tactile reminder of his success.

"Easy money," he muttered, his lips curving into a smirk. The thrill of the transaction coursed through him, a heady mix of adrenaline and greed that quickened his steps.

Billy glanced at his watch, a cheap knockoff that belied his newfound wealth. It was time to celebrate. He hailed a cab, relishing the luxury of not having to take public transport.

"The Gilded Leaf," he instructed the driver, naming an upscale restaurant he'd only dreamed of visiting before.

As the cab weaved through traffic, Billy's mind raced with possibilities. "This is just the beginning," he thought, his eyes gleaming with anticipation.

The restaurant's opulent facade loomed before him. Billy straightened his posture, adopted an air of casual affluence, and strode in.

"Table for one," he said to the maître d', flashing a winning smile.

Seated at a corner table, Billy perused the menu, his eyes widening at the prices. "What the hell," he muttered. "I've earned this."

When the waiter approached, Billy ordered with practiced ease. "I'll start with the foie gras, followed by the Wagyu ribeye. And a bottle of your finest red."

As he waited, Billy savored the atmosphere, the clink of fine china, the murmur of well-heeled patrons. "I could get used to this," he mused, already plotting his next move.

Billy twirled the stem of his wine glass, the rich Bordeaux catching the light. His eyes unfocused, mind drifting to his next target.

"It's all about the routine," he muttered under his breath, methodically cutting into his steak. "Find the weak link, exploit it."

A couple at the next table glanced his way. Billy flashed them a disarming smile, the mask of normalcy slipping effortlessly into place.

"Lovely evening, isn't it?" he said cheerfully, before turning back to his meal.

As he chewed, Billy mentally ticked off his criteria. "Elderly, isolated, valuable possessions," he thought. "And always, always establish trust first."

The waiter approached. "Will sir be having dessert?"

Billy's lips curled into a predatory grin. "Why not? I'm feeling indulgent tonight."

As he savored the rich chocolate mousse, Billy's thoughts sharpened. "Time to get back to work," he decided. "Can't rest on my laurels."

Settling his bill with a generous tip, Billy stepped out into the cool night air. His modest apartment beckoned, a stark contrast to the evening's opulence.

Inside, Billy shrugged off his jacket and made a beeline for his cluttered desk. Newspapers and community newsletters littered the surface, a treasure trove of information.

"Let's see who's left this world recently," he murmured, fingers tracing the obituary columns. His eyes narrowed as a familiar name caught his attention.

"Well, well," Billy whispered, a slow smile spreading across his face. "Isn't this interesting?"

Billy's eyes locked onto the name: Edna Winters, 91. His pulse quickened as he scanned the details.

"Golden Years Home," he muttered, scribbling furiously in his notebook. "Perfect."

He leaned back, tapping his pen against his teeth. "Ninety-one. Likely has some valuable trinkets. No mention of family."

Billy's mind raced, piecing together a plan. He reached for his laptop, fingers flying over the keys as he pulled up the Golden Years website.

"Security measures?" he mused aloud. "Time to take a closer look."

The next morning, Billy eased his nondescript sedan into a parking spot across from Golden Years. He adjusted his baseball cap, eyes scanning the perimeter.

"Cameras at the main entrance," he noted mentally. "Side door looks promising."

He drummed his fingers on the steering wheel. "How many staff on duty? Shift changes?"

A delivery van pulled up to the back. Billy's eyes narrowed, watching the driver's casual interaction with security.

"There's my in," he thought, a slow smile spreading across his face.

He jotted down notes, his handwriting precise despite his excitement. "Maintenance uniform. Maybe plumbing issue?"

Billy's gaze drifted to an open second-floor window. "Easy access, if needed."

He settled deeper into his seat, prepared for a long day of observation. "Patience," he reminded himself. "This is just the beginning."

Billy stepped out of his car, adjusting his worn denim jacket and baseball cap. He merged seamlessly into the flow of visitors entering

Golden Years, his posture relaxed, his gait unhurried. A nurse brushed past him, and he offered a friendly nod.

"Afternoon," he said, his voice warm and unremarkable.

The nurse smiled back, already focused on her next task. Billy suppressed a smirk. Invisible, just how he liked it.

He strolled along the winding path, eyes darting to each window. Elderly faces peered out, some vacant, others curious. Billy's gaze lingered on a second-floor room, where a frail woman with silver hair sat in a rocking chair.

"Edna?" he wondered, his heart rate picking up.

A groundskeeper approached, pushing a wheelbarrow. Billy gestured at the immaculate lawn.

"Place looks great," he commented casually. "You guys hiring?"

The man shrugged. "Always short-staffed. You looking for work?"

Billy chuckled, shaking his head. "Nah, just curious. My aunt's thinking of moving in."

As the groundskeeper moved on, Billy's mind raced. A job here would provide the perfect cover. He filed the information away, continuing his circuit of the building.

His eyes flicked from window to window, cataloging faces, routines, potential weaknesses. But always, his thoughts returned to Edna.

"Soon," he promised himself, his fingers twitching with anticipation. "Very soon."

Billy's pace slowed as he neared the entrance again. His mind shifted gears, rehearsing the routine he'd perfected over countless cons.

"Just need to check the wiring in 203," he muttered under his breath, practicing his maintenance man persona. His face transformed, adopting a look of mild concern. "Shouldn't take more than a few minutes, ma'am."

He flexed his fingers, imagining the feel of Edna's jewelry. His heartbeat quickened, a predator's anticipation.

A car door slammed nearby. Billy's head snapped up, instantly alert. An elderly couple shuffled towards the entrance, the man supporting his wife.

"Need a hand?" Billy called out, his voice warm and helpful.

The old man waved him off. "We're fine, son. Thank you."

Billy nodded, watching them disappear inside. He filed away their faces, potential future targets.

The sun dipped lower, casting long shadows across the manicured lawn. Billy stood motionless, his eyes fixed on the building. Golden light glinted off the windows, but he saw only opportunity within.

"One more day," he thought, his pulse quickening. "Then showtime."

He turned away, forcing himself to walk at a casual pace. But inside, every nerve tingled with the thrill of the impending hunt.

Chapter 5

Billy Thompson adjusted his worn baseball cap as he approached apartment 302. The faded name plate read "E. Winters" in tarnished brass letters. He took a deep breath, shoulders relaxing as he slipped into character.

Knock knock knock.

"Maintenance," Billy called out in a cheerful tone. "Just here to check on that leaky faucet, ma'am."

Shuffling footsteps approached from inside. Billy's pulse quickened, but his face remained placid. The door opened a crack, revealing a wary blue eye.

"I don't remember calling about any leak," Edna said, her voice quavering.

Billy flashed a disarming smile. "Oh, it was your neighbor downstairs who reported it. Building manager asked me to take a look, just in case. Better safe than sorry, right?"

Edna hesitated. Billy could almost see the gears turning in her mind. He kept his posture loose, projecting an aura of casual friendliness.

"Well, I suppose it wouldn't hurt to check," Edna said finally. The door swung open.

"I appreciate it, ma'am," Billy said, stepping inside. His eyes darted around, cataloging valuables. "Kitchen this way?"

"Yes, just through there," Edna replied, gesturing vaguely. "Let me get my glasses so I can show you..."

As she turned away, Billy's smile faded. His hand slipped into his pocket. Just a few more seconds and she'd never see it coming.

Billy moved with lightning speed. In one fluid motion, he snatched a decorative pillow from the nearby couch and lunged at Edna. His arm wrapped around her frail body, pinning her arms to her sides as he pressed the pillow firmly over her face.

"Shh, shh," he whispered, his voice devoid of emotion. "It'll be over soon."

Edna's muffled screams were barely audible through the thick fabric. Her legs kicked feebly, her body twisting in a desperate attempt to break free. Billy's grip remained iron-clad, his eyes cold and calculating as he watched her struggle.

Is this taking longer than usual? he wondered, glancing at his watch. Come on, come on.

After what felt like an eternity, Edna's movements began to slow. Her arms went limp, then her legs. Billy maintained the pressure for another full minute, just to be sure.

Finally, he released his hold, letting Edna's lifeless body slump to the floor. He didn't spare her a second glance as he turned his attention to the task at hand.

"Now, where do you keep the good stuff, Edna?" Billy muttered, his eyes scanning the room.

He moved with practiced efficiency, opening drawers and rifling through cabinets. A small jewelry box on the dresser yielded a pair of pearl earrings and a gold locket. Billy pocketed them without hesitation.

In the living room, he spotted a collection of antique silver spoons. Valuable, but too bulky. He settled for prying out the few gems inlaid in the handles.

As he worked, Billy's mind raced. This is getting easier every time. Maybe I should branch out, try some of the fancier retirement communities. Bigger risk, but bigger payoff.

He paused at a framed photo of Edna with what looked like grandchildren. For a brief moment, something akin to guilt flashed across his face. Then it was gone, replaced by his usual mask of indifference.

"Sorry, kids," he said with a shrug. "Grandma's helping fund my early retirement."

Billy's gaze lingered on the framed photo, his fingers tracing the edge. A twisted smile played across his lips as he plucked it from the wall.

"You know what?" he mused aloud. "I think I'll keep this."

He slipped the photo from its frame, folding it carefully before tucking it into his pocket. The thrill of this new habit sent a shiver down his spine.

"A little memento," Billy chuckled. "To remember our time together, Edna."

His eyes darted around the room, seeking more personal treasures. A delicate porcelain figurine caught his attention – a ballerina, arms gracefully extended.

"Perfect," he whispered, wrapping it in a handkerchief before adding it to his growing collection.

Satisfied with his haul, Billy straightened his maintenance uniform and headed for the door. As he stepped out, he glanced at his watch.

"Time to pay Herbert a visit," he muttered, a confident smirk spreading across his face.

Twenty minutes later, Billy stood before Herbert Grayson's door, his posture relaxed, smile disarming. He knocked, the sound echoing in the quiet hallway.

"Mr. Grayson?" he called out. "Maintenance. Just need to check your smoke detectors."

Billy's heart raced with anticipation, but his exterior remained calm. This is too easy, he thought. They trust the uniform every time.

The door creaked open, revealing Herbert's weathered face.

"Smoke detectors, you say?" Herbert squinted suspiciously.

Billy's smile widened. "Just a routine check, sir. Won't take but a minute."

Billy stepped into Herbert's apartment, his eyes quickly scanning the room. The old man shuffled behind him, closing the door with a soft click.

"Let's make this quick," Herbert grumbled. "I've got a program coming on soon."

"Of course, sir," Billy replied, his voice dripping with false sincerity. "I'll be out of your hair in no time."

As Herbert turned his back, Billy's demeanor shifted. In one fluid motion, he pulled a plastic bag from his pocket and lunged forward. The attack was swift, precise – a testament to his growing skill.

Herbert's muffled cries were short-lived. Billy held firm, his face a mask of cold determination as he watched the life drain from the old man's eyes.

"Easier every time," Billy muttered, lowering Herbert's lifeless body to the floor.

He glanced at his watch. Five minutes. A new record.

Billy's hands moved methodically as he searched the apartment. Jewelry, cash, anything of value disappeared into his pockets.

"What have we here?" he mused, picking up a small wooden box. Inside, a collection of war medals glinted in the dim light.

"Sorry, old timer. These are coming with me."

As he prepared to leave, Billy caught his reflection in a mirror. He adjusted his cap, smoothed his shirt, and plastered on a friendly smile.

"Just another day at work," he chuckled to himself.

Billy stepped out of Herbert's apartment, closing the door gently behind him. He nodded politely to a passing resident, his demeanor betraying nothing of the horror he'd left behind.

"All set in there?" the elderly woman asked.

"Right as rain, ma'am," Billy replied with a wink. "Have a wonderful evening."

He strolled down the hallway, whistling softly, blending seamlessly into the everyday world – just another maintenance man finishing his shift.

Detective Jake Miller hunched over his desk, brow furrowed as he sifted through a stack of death reports. The harsh fluorescent light cast shadows across his face, accentuating the fatigue etched into his features.

"Damn it," he muttered, reaching for his coffee. "This can't be a coincidence."

His eyes darted from one report to another, mind racing. Six deaths in three different retirement communities over the past two months. All ruled as natural causes, but something didn't sit right.

Jake's partner, Davis, approached. "Still chasing ghosts, Miller?"

"These aren't ghosts, Davis," Jake replied, his voice tight with frustration. "Look at the pattern. The timing, the similarities in how they were found."

Davis shrugged. "Old folks die, Jake. It's what they do."

Jake's jaw clenched. He stood abruptly, gathering the reports. "I'm taking this to Captain Reeves."

In Reeves' office, Jake laid out his suspicions, his words rapid-fire and urgent. "Sir, I believe we're dealing with a serial killer targeting the elderly."

Reeves leaned back, skepticism clear in his eyes. "Based on what, exactly? Natural causes aren't exactly smoking guns, Miller."

"It's the pattern, sir," Jake insisted, spreading the reports across the desk. "The clustered timeframes, the lack of signs of forced entry—"

"Because there was no forced entry," Reeves interrupted. "These were all ruled as natural deaths by the ME."

Jake's fists clenched at his sides. "With all due respect, sir, I think we're missing something crucial here. If we don't act—"

"Enough, Miller," Reeves cut him off, his tone final. "I appreciate your dedication, but we can't waste resources chasing shadows. Unless you bring me concrete evidence, this discussion is over."

As Jake left the office, his mind raced. They're wrong, all of them, he thought. I know there's more to this. I have to find a way to prove it before anyone else dies.

Jake's fingers flew across the keyboard, the harsh glow of the computer screen illuminating his determined face. He'd commandeered an empty interrogation room, transforming it into his personal war room. Pinned to the walls were maps, timelines, and victim profiles.

"There has to be a connection," he muttered, eyes darting between his notes and the screen. He pulled up another death certificate, scanning for details others might have missed.

A knock at the door startled him. "Miller, you still here?" It was Davis, peering in with a mix of concern and exasperation.

"Just following up on some leads," Jake replied, not looking up.

Davis sighed. "Jake, man, you need to let this go. You're seeing ghosts."

Jake's head snapped up, eyes blazing. "These aren't ghosts, Davis. These are real people. Vulnerable people who deserved better than to die alone and afraid."

"Look, I get it—"

"No, you don't," Jake cut him off, standing. "Something's happening here, and I'm going to prove it."

As Davis left, shaking his head, Jake turned back to his work. He'd compile every scrap of evidence, connect every dot, no matter how long it took.

Across town, Billy lounged in his threadbare armchair, idly flipping through a stack of community newspapers. His eyes gleamed as he circled another obituary.

"Well, well," he murmured, a cold smile playing on his lips. "Looks like Mrs. Abernathy just lost her husband. Bet she could use some... companionship."

He chuckled, already imagining the trinkets and cash stashed away in her home. The thrill of the hunt coursed through him, stronger than ever.

"They make it so easy," Billy mused, stretching languidly. "No one even bats an eye. It's like I'm invisible."

His fingers brushed the small box on the side table, filled with his growing collection of trophies. Each item a reminder of his victories, his cleverness.

"Time to pay Mrs. Abernathy a visit," he decided, standing. "After all, a good neighbor should offer condolences."

Jake's fist clenched around his pen, knuckles whitening. He stared at the crime board, a web of red strings connecting photos and notes. The faces of the elderly victims haunted him, their eyes seeming to plead for justice.

"I won't let you down," he whispered fiercely. "I swear it."

He grabbed his jacket, determination etched in every line of his face. As he strode out, Jake's partner called after him.

"Where you headed, Miller?"

"To find the truth," Jake shot back, not breaking stride. "Even if I have to dig it up with my bare hands."

The precinct door slammed behind him, the sound echoing his resolve.

Across town, Billy sauntered into Hal's Pawn, a small velvet pouch jingling in his pocket. The shop owner's eyes narrowed suspiciously.

"Back so soon, Thompson?"

Billy flashed an easy grin. "What can I say? It's yard sale season."

He emptied the pouch onto the counter – a tangle of gold chains and rings glinting under the fluorescent lights.

"Nice haul," Hal muttered, examining a locket. "Where'd you say you got these?"

"Does it matter?" Billy's tone remained light, but his eyes held a warning. "You gonna buy 'em or not?"

As Hal counted out cash, Billy's mind raced to his next target. The thrill of the hunt, the promise of more treasures to come – it was intoxicating.

"Pleasure doing business," he drawled, pocketing the money. Outside, Billy whistled a cheerful tune, blending seamlessly into the afternoon crowd.

Chapter 6

The fluorescent lights buzzed overhead as Billy shuffled through the police station doors, his wrists chafing against the cold metal handcuffs. Two burly officers flanked him, their grip firm on his arms. He kept his eyes down, studying the scuffed linoleum floor.

Breathe. Stay calm. This is just a setback.

Billy forced his shoulders to relax, plastering on a neutral expression. Inside, frustration churned. How had they caught onto him so quickly? He'd been careful, meticulous even. No matter. He'd find a way out of this.

"Step this way," the officer on his left grunted, steering him toward the booking desk.

Billy complied, his worn sneakers squeaking on the floor. "Sure thing, officer. Happy to cooperate."

As they approached the desk, Billy felt eyes on him. He glanced up, meeting the sharp gaze of a dark-haired woman in uniform. Officer Ortiz, her nameplate read. Something in her piercing stare made Billy's skin prickle.

Stay cool. Don't let her rattle you.

He flashed Officer Ortiz a friendly smile and nod. "Evening, ma'am."

Samantha's eyes narrowed, her posture stiffening. "Evening," she replied curtly.

Billy turned back to the booking officer, answering questions in a steady voice. But he could still feel Samantha's gaze boring into him.

What's her deal? She can't know anything. I've never seen her before.

As Billy recited his address, he heard Samantha murmur to a colleague. "Something's not right with this guy. I can feel it."

Billy's heart rate kicked up a notch. He forced himself to keep his expression neutral, his tone light as he continued answering questions. But inside, his mind raced.

I need to be extra careful around that one. She could be trouble.

The fluorescent lights buzzed overhead as Samantha shut the interrogation room door behind her. She took a seat across from Billy, her posture rigid, eyes laser-focused on his face.

"So, Mr. Thompson," Samantha began, her tone crisp. "Want to tell me about your whereabouts last night?"

Billy leaned back, his posture relaxed, a easy smile playing on his lips. "Sure thing, Officer Ortiz. I was at home, watching the game. Brewers vs. Cubs. Helluva match-up."

Samantha's pen scratched across her notepad. "Anyone who can verify that?"

"'Fraid not," Billy shrugged, his voice tinged with mock regret. "Bachelor life, you know how it is."

She doesn't buy it, Billy thought, noticing the slight tightening around Samantha's eyes. Gotta sell this harder.

"Look," he continued, leaning forward conspiratorially. "I get why I'm here. Old lady gets robbed, cops round up the usual suspects. But I swear, I had nothing to do with it."

Samantha's gaze didn't waver. "We have witnesses placing someone matching your description near Mrs. Goldstein's home."

Billy's heart raced, but he kept his voice steady. "Lots of guys look like me, Officer. Average height, brown hair. I'm not exactly unique."

"True," Samantha conceded, her tone flat. "But not many work as caregivers in that neighborhood."

Shit. Billy's mind raced. She's connecting dots I didn't even know existed.

He forced a chuckle. "Used to work there. Left that job months ago. Wasn't my scene, you know?"

Samantha's eyes narrowed. "And yet, you're still in the area."

"It's a nice neighborhood," Billy countered, shrugging. "Good coffee shop on the corner. Why move?"

As he spoke, Billy could see the gears turning in Samantha's head. Her questions grew more pointed, her tone sharper. He matched her intensity with increased friendliness, peppering his responses with self-deprecating jokes and charming anecdotes.

But beneath his calm exterior, Billy's nerves were fraying. She's not letting up. How much does she actually know?

The heavy metal door clanged shut behind Billy as he stepped out of the police station, inhaling deeply. The crisp night air filled his lungs, carrying with it the promise of freedom and opportunity. He adjusted his stained baseball cap, a smile playing at the corners of his mouth.

"Thanks for the hospitality, boys," Billy called over his shoulder, his voice dripping with mock sincerity. "Let's not do this again sometime, yeah?"

As he strode away, his mind was already racing. Gotta switch things up. Can't risk another close call like that.

He shoved his hands in his pockets, hunching his shoulders against the chill. The streetlights cast long shadows, perfect for concealing his true intentions from any prying eyes.

"Private homes," he muttered to himself. "Less security, more isolated. Easier in, easier out."

Billy's pace quickened as excitement bubbled up inside him. This setback was just a chance to refine his approach. He'd always been good at adapting, at finding the path of least resistance.

"Those retirement communities were getting too hot anyway," he reasoned internally. "Too many nosy neighbors, too much gossip. But a quiet street? A standalone house? Now that's got potential."

He pictured the layout of the nearby neighborhoods in his mind, mentally cataloging potential targets. The thrill of the hunt sent a shiver down his spine that had nothing to do with the cold.

"Just gotta be smarter," Billy whispered, his eyes gleaming with renewed determination. "Blend in better, maybe pose as a handyman or delivery guy. They'll never see me coming."

As he disappeared into the shadows, Billy's mind raced with possibilities. The brief stint in jail hadn't broken him – it had only made him more determined to succeed.

Eleanor Hughes shuffled down the sidewalk, her arms laden with grocery bags. Her wispy white hair fluttered in the breeze as she paused to catch her breath, leaning heavily on her cane.

"Oh, these old bones," she muttered, adjusting her grip on the plastic handles. "Should've asked that nice young man at the store to help carry these."

Unbeknownst to Eleanor, a figure lurked in the shadows across the street. Billy's eyes narrowed as he watched the elderly woman's slow progress, his mind already calculating.

"Perfect," he thought, a smirk playing at the corners of his mouth. "Isolated, vulnerable, probably has a lifetime of savings stashed away."

Eleanor fumbled with her house keys, the grocery bags swinging precariously.

Billy's fingers twitched with anticipation. "Easy pickings," he mused. "Just gotta time it right."

He slouched against a nearby tree, feigning casualness as he kept Eleanor in his peripheral vision. His nondescript clothing blended seamlessly with the suburban backdrop.

"Excuse me, ma'am?" Billy called out, his voice dripping with false concern. "Need a hand with those bags?"

Eleanor turned, startled. "Oh! That's very kind of you, young man, but I wouldn't want to trouble you."

Billy's predatory gaze softened into a mask of friendliness. "No trouble at all," he insisted, already moving towards her. "Happy to help a neighbor."

As he approached, Billy's mind raced. "Play it cool," he reminded himself. "Gain her trust. The payoff will be worth it."

Billy's eyes darted around Eleanor's property, taking in every detail. The overgrown hedges, the peeling paint, the lack of security cameras. His confidence surged. This was perfect.

"Thanks again for your help," Eleanor called from her porch, waving.

Billy nodded, flashing a disarming smile. "Anytime, ma'am." He turned away, his friendly facade dropping instantly. "Too easy," he muttered under his breath.

Across town, fluorescent lights hummed in the precinct as Officer Samantha Ortiz paced, her ponytail swinging with each turn.

"I'm telling you, Jake, something's not right about this guy," she insisted, facing her partner.

Detective Miller leaned against his desk, arms crossed. "I hear you, Sam, but we need more than a gut feeling."

Samantha's eyes flashed. "You didn't see him in that interrogation room. The way he answered everything... it was too smooth."

"Maybe he's just cooperative," Jake suggested, but his tone lacked conviction.

"Or maybe he's playing us," Samantha countered. She grabbed a file, flipping it open. "Look at his priors. Petty theft, fraud... he's escalating."

Jake rubbed his beard thoughtfully. "What are you thinking?"

Samantha slammed the file shut. "I'm thinking we need to keep eyes on him. He's going to slip up, and when he does, I want to be there."

"Sam," Jake's voice softened, "we can't surveil him without cause."

"Then we find cause," she snapped, determination etched in every line of her face.

Billy watched from his parked car as Eleanor's porch light flickered off. His fingers drummed the steering wheel, mind churning with possibilities. "Routine," he murmured. "That's the key."

He'd spent days observing Eleanor's habits. The 7 AM walk to collect her newspaper. Tuesdays and Fridays at the senior center. Sunday afternoons tending her small garden.

"Predictable," Billy smirked. "Just how I like 'em."

He reached for his notebook, jotting down ideas. "Maintenance man? Nah, too obvious." His pen paused. "What about a volunteer? Meals on Wheels, maybe?"

Billy's eyes gleamed as the plan took shape. He'd need a new outfit, some fake credentials. Nothing he hadn't done before.

"Gotta play the long game this time," he reminded himself. "No rush. Build trust."

A car passed, headlights sweeping across Billy's face. He instinctively ducked, then chuckled at his own paranoia.

"Relax," he told himself. "You're just a concerned citizen checking on a neighbor."

But as Billy started his car, a chill ran down his spine. He glanced back at Eleanor's darkened house, suddenly aware of the weight of his actions.

"It's just business," he muttered, but the words rang hollow in the empty car.

Billy pulled away, melting into the night. But the image of Eleanor's vulnerable home lingered, a silent promise of what was to come.

Chapter 7

Billy Thompson ambled through the sun-dappled paths of Peaceful Pines Retirement Community, his stained baseball cap pulled low. A gentle breeze ruffled the leaves, carrying the scent of freshly mown grass. Perfect day for a stroll, he mused, eyes darting from porch to porch.

"Morning, sir!" he called out cheerfully to an elderly man watering flowers. The old timer waved back absently.

Billy's gaze lingered on the man's gold watch glinting in the sunlight. Too risky, he decided. Too visible.

He rounded a corner, spotting a modestly kept bungalow with drawn curtains. Bingo.

Heart quickening, Billy approached the door marked "E. Hughes" and rapped three times. Showtime.

The door creaked open, revealing a frail woman with wispy white hair.

"Can I help you?" she asked hesitantly.

Billy flashed his most disarming smile. "Mrs. Hughes? I'm from maintenance. Just need to check your smoke alarms."

"Oh, I don't recall..."

"It'll only take a minute, ma'am." He held up a toolbox prop. "Safety first, right?"

Eleanor Hughes hesitated, then nodded. "Well, alright then. Come in."

As she turned, Billy's friendly demeanor evaporated. In one fluid motion, he stepped inside, shut the door, and grabbed a decorative pillow from a nearby chair.

Eleanor barely had time to gasp before Billy was on her, clamping the pillow over her face with terrifying strength. She struggled weakly, her muffled cries fading as Billy pressed down harder.

Just a little longer, he thought grimly. It'll be over soon.

Billy's eyes scanned the room methodically as Eleanor's body went limp. He gently lowered her to the floor, arranging her limbs in a natural sleeping position on the floral patterned couch.

"Sorry, darlin'," he muttered, his tone oddly casual. "Just business, you understand."

He moved swiftly through the apartment, practiced hands opening drawers and rifling through jewelry boxes. A pearl necklace, a few gold rings, some cash from a purse – all disappeared into his pockets with quiet efficiency.

Pausing at a framed photo, Billy's eyes narrowed. "Granddaughter?" he mused. "Shame she won't be visitin' anymore."

A twinge of... something flickered across his face, quickly replaced by cool detachment. He shook his head, refocusing on the task at hand.

Fifteen minutes later, Billy emerged from Eleanor's apartment, toolbox in hand. He nodded politely to a passing resident, then consulted a crumpled list.

"Thomas Blackwell, 82, widower," he murmured. "Unit 14B. Time to get to work."

Billy's stride was purposeful as he approached the maintenance shed. Swapping his baseball cap for a official-looking uniform hat, he grabbed a ladder and headed towards Thomas's building.

Knocking firmly on 14B's door, Billy called out, "Maintenance! Need to check your smoke detectors, sir."

A gruff voice responded, "Didn't hear anything about that."

Billy's tone remained friendly, but his eyes hardened. "Just a routine check, Mr. Blackwell. Won't take but a minute of your time."

The door opened, revealing Thomas – white-haired, slightly stooped, but with sharp eyes that studied Billy warily.

"Mind if I come in?" Billy asked, flashing his disarming smile. "Gotta make sure you're all safe and sound in here."

Thomas hesitated, then nodded reluctantly. "I suppose so. But make it quick."

As Billy entered, his fingers tightened imperceptibly on the ladder. One way or another, he thought grimly, this would indeed be quick.

Billy's heart raced with exhilaration as he approached Margaret Foster's door. His hands, steady and sure, adjusted the name tag on his uniform. He knocked, three sharp raps.

"Coming!" a frail voice called from inside.

Billy's lips curled into a cold smile. "Maintenance, ma'am. Here to check your thermostat."

The door creaked open, revealing Margaret's wizened face. "Oh, I didn't expect anyone today."

"Just a routine check," Billy replied smoothly, shouldering his way in. "Won't take but a moment."

As the door clicked shut behind him, Billy's demeanor shifted. His movements became precise, calculated. He scanned the room, noting valuables with practiced efficiency.

"Now, Mrs. Foster," he said, voice low and menacing, "let's make this easy, shall we?"

Margaret's eyes widened in fear. "What—"

Billy's hand clamped over her mouth, cutting off her cry. "Shh, shh. It'll be over soon."

As he carried out his grim task, Billy's thoughts raced. This is too easy. They're all so trusting. So vulnerable.

Fifteen minutes later, he emerged from the apartment, pockets heavier, expression neutral. He turned to lock the door and froze.

"Oh, hello there!" chirped a voice behind him.

Billy's pulse quickened, but he forced a friendly smile as he turned. "Afternoon, ma'am."

An elderly woman stood in the hallway, eyeing him curiously. "I don't think I've seen you around before. Are you new?"

"Just filling in today," Billy replied smoothly. "Checking on a few units. How're you doing this fine day?"

The woman beamed. "Oh, can't complain. Say, have you seen Margaret? We were supposed to have tea."

Billy's mind raced. "I'm afraid Mrs. Foster wasn't feeling well. Said she needed to rest."

"Oh dear," the woman clucked sympathetically. "I'll check on her later then."

Billy nodded, inching towards the exit. "You're a good friend. Take care now."

As he walked away, Billy's face hardened. Too close. Need to be more careful. But the thrill... it's worth the risk.

Billy approached Ruth Coleman's door, his steps purposeful, his demeanor calm. He knocked, a disarming smile already in place.

"Who is it?" called a quavering voice from inside.

"Maintenance, ma'am. Just need to check your smoke detectors."

The door opened, revealing Ruth's frail form. Billy's eyes darted over her, assessing. Weak. Alone. Perfect.

"Oh, come in," Ruth said, stepping back. "I wasn't expecting anyone."

Billy entered, his movements fluid and practiced. "Won't take but a moment, ma'am."

As he closed the door, his façade dropped. In one swift motion, he grabbed Ruth, his hand clamping over her mouth. "No noise now," he hissed.

Ruth's eyes bulged with terror, her feeble struggles no match for Billy's strength. He worked quickly, efficiently, his face a mask of cold indifference.

Moments later, Billy stood over Ruth's lifeless body, breathing heavily. Easier every time, he thought, a thrill coursing through him. He pocketed her jewelry, his movements precise and unhurried.

As he left, he straightened his cap, his mask of normalcy sliding back into place.

Across town, Detective Jake Miller hunched over his desk, brow furrowed in concentration. Scattered reports covered the surface, each detailing another elderly death.

"Damn it," Jake muttered, running a hand through his hair. "What am I missing?"

He picked up another file, scanning it quickly. "Natural causes, again. But something's not right. Too many in such a short time."

Jake stood, pacing the small office. "There's got to be a connection. But what?"

He turned back to the desk, determination etched on his face. "I'm not letting this go. Someone's preying on these people, and I'm going to find out who."

Jake's fingers flew across the keyboard, his eyes darting between the screen and the stack of files beside him. He'd been at it for hours, fueled by coffee and an unshakable sense that something was terribly wrong.

"Come on, give me something," he muttered, scrolling through another medical examiner's report. His jaw clenched as he read the familiar phrase: "Natural causes."

Jake leaned back, rubbing his tired eyes. The faces of the elderly victims flashed through his mind, igniting a surge of protective anger. "I won't let you down," he promised silently.

A knock at his office door jolted him from his thoughts. "Come in," Jake called, straightening up.

The door opened, revealing a woman with shoulder-length blonde hair and piercing blue eyes. She carried herself with a quiet authority that immediately caught Jake's attention.

"Detective Miller?" she asked, her voice calm but tinged with urgency.

Jake nodded, standing to greet her. "That's me. And you are?"

"Evelyn Davis. I'm an administrator at Sunnyside Retirement Community." She extended her hand, which Jake shook firmly. "I hope

I'm not interrupting, but I need to speak with you about something important."

Jake's investigator instincts kicked into high gear. "Not at all, Ms. Davis. Please, have a seat." He gestured to the chair across from his desk. "What seems to be the problem?"

Evelyn sat, her posture straight, hands folded in her lap. "It's about the deaths at our community. There have been... too many."

Jake leaned forward, his interest piqued. "I'm listening."

"In the past month alone, we've lost five residents," Evelyn continued, her voice steady but laced with concern. "All ruled as natural causes, but..." She hesitated.

"But?" Jake prompted, sensing her unease.

Evelyn met his gaze, her blue eyes filled with a mix of compassion and determination. "But it doesn't feel right. These were healthy, active seniors. And the timing, it's just... off."

Jake nodded, his mind racing. Could this be the break he'd been looking for? "I appreciate you coming forward, Ms. Davis. Can you tell me more about these residents?"

As Evelyn began to speak, Jake grabbed a notepad, his pen poised. Finally, he thought, a lead. And maybe, just maybe, a chance to stop whoever was preying on the vulnerable before they struck again.

Jake scribbled furiously as Evelyn recounted the details, her calm demeanor belying the gravity of her words. "Each victim was found in their bed, seemingly peaceful. No signs of struggle."

"And you're certain there's no medical explanation?" Jake pressed, his brow furrowed.

Evelyn's eyes flashed with quiet authority. "Detective, I've worked with the elderly for twenty years. This isn't normal."

Jake leaned back, tapping his pen against the desk. Something sinister was definitely at play. "Ms. Davis, have you noticed anyone new around the community? Any unfamiliar faces?"

"We have strict security protocols," Evelyn replied, her tone measured. "But... now that you mention it, there was a maintenance worker I didn't recognize last week."

Jake's pulse quickened. "Can you describe him?"

As Evelyn spoke, Jake's suspicion grew. This was no coincidence.

Meanwhile, across town, Billy approached George Simmons' door, his heart racing with anticipation. The baseball cap pulled low couldn't hide the glint in his eyes.

"Mr. Simmons?" Billy called, his voice a perfect blend of concern and friendliness. "Maintenance. Got a report of a leak."

The door creaked open, revealing George's weathered face. "Leak? I didn't call about any leak."

Billy's smile widened, predatory. "Better safe than sorry, sir. Mind if I take a look?"

As George hesitated, Billy's fingers twitched, ready to spring into action. The thrill of the hunt coursed through him. He was unstoppable, invincible. And George Simmons was his next prize.

Billy slipped out of George Simmons' apartment, his pockets heavy with stolen treasures. The weight of the gold watch and diamond ring felt satisfying against his thigh as he strode down the hallway, a spring in his step.

"Afternoon, Mr. Thompson," a passing resident called out.

Billy tipped his cap, flashing an easy smile. "Beautiful day, isn't it?" he replied, his voice warm and unassuming.

As he pushed through the lobby doors, sunlight glinted off his stolen bounty. Billy inhaled deeply, savoring the rush of another successful heist.

"Too easy," he muttered, fishing car keys from his pocket. "They'll never catch on."

Across town, Jake Miller hunched over his desk, surrounded by case files. His eyes burned from hours of scrutiny, but he couldn't shake the nagging feeling in his gut.

"What am I missing?" he growled, rubbing his temples.

The phone rang, jarring him from his thoughts. "Miller," he barked.

"Detective, it's Evelyn Davis," came the calm voice on the other end. "I've been reviewing our records. There's something you need to see."

Jake's pulse quickened. "I'm on my way," he said, already reaching for his jacket.

As he rushed out, Jake's mind raced. No hard evidence yet, but his instincts screamed that they were close. Whatever was happening at that retirement community, he'd get to the bottom of it. No matter what it took.

Jake's fingers drummed against the steering wheel as he navigated through traffic, his mind churning. The pieces were there, just out of reach. He could feel it.

"Come on, come on," he muttered, willing the lights to change.

His phone buzzed. A text from Evelyn: "Found employee records. Possible connection."

Jake's jaw clenched. "Gotcha," he whispered.

At the precinct, he burst through the doors, making a beeline for his partner's desk.

"Rodriguez," he called out. "I need everything we've got on recent hires at Sunnyside Retirement."

Rodriguez looked up, startled. "What's the angle?"

Jake leaned in, voice low. "Pattern. Deaths spike, new maintenance guy shows up. Could be nothing, but—"

"Or it could be everything," Rodriguez finished, already typing.

Jake nodded, his eyes blazing with determination. "We're close. I can feel it."

Across town, oblivious to the net closing around him, Billy whistled as he appraised his latest haul. The old man's Rolex glinted in the dim light of his apartment.

"Not bad, old timer," he chuckled. "This'll fetch a pretty penny."

His phone chimed. Another job. Billy grinned, already imagining the score.

"One more," he mused. "Then I'm out. They'll never know what hit 'em."

As night fell, two men prepared. One to strike again, the other to stop him. The clock was ticking.

Chapter 8

Billy Thompson adjusted his faded baseball cap and plastered on his most disarming smile as he approached apartment 3B. His heart raced beneath the threadbare uniform shirt, but his movements remained casual, unhurried. Just another day on the job.

He rapped his knuckles against the weathered wood. "Maintenance," he called out, voice pitched to carry through the door without seeming overly eager.

The lock clicked, and the door swung open to reveal a diminutive woman with a shock of white hair. Her piercing blue eyes swept over him, sharp and assessing.

"I don't recall putting in a maintenance request," Gertrude said, her tone crisp.

Billy's smile didn't waver. "Just doing routine checks, ma'am. Won't take but a minute of your time."

Gertrude's eyes narrowed slightly. "At this hour?"

"Building manager's orders," Billy lied smoothly. "Trying to catch everyone before the weekend."

He watched as Gertrude hesitated, weighing her options. Come on, lady. Let me in.

"Well, I suppose if it's quick," Gertrude relented, stepping back from the doorway.

Billy nodded gratefully, slipping past her into the apartment. "I appreciate it, ma'am. Won't be long at all."

As the door clicked shut behind him, Billy felt a familiar thrill of anticipation. Another mark, another score. And this one looked promising.

Billy's eyes darted around the room, cataloging potential targets. A glint of gold caught his attention—an ornate picture frame on the mantle. Antique, probably valuable. His gaze swept over a collection of delicate porcelain figurines. Easy to pocket, easier to fence.

"So, what exactly are you checking?" Gertrude's voice cut through his mental inventory.

Billy forced his focus back to the present. "Just making sure all the electrical is up to code, ma'am." He moved toward a nearby lamp, adopting an air of professional scrutiny. "These older buildings can have some tricky wiring."

Gertrude huffed. "I've lived here for thirty years without any electrical issues."

"Better safe than sorry," Billy replied, his tone carefully modulated to convey reassurance. He bent to examine the lamp's cord, all the while acutely aware of Gertrude's position in the room. Just a few more moments of this charade.

"You know," Gertrude mused, "you remind me of my grandson. He's about your age, works in construction."

Billy straightened, offering a practiced chuckle. "Is that right? Small world." His hand brushed against the pillow on the nearby armchair. Perfect. Now or never.

In one fluid motion, Billy snatched up the pillow and spun to face Gertrude. Her bright eyes widened in shock as his friendly facade crumbled, revealing the cold, hard intent beneath.

"I'm sorry about this," he muttered, more to himself than to her. Then he lunged, pillow outstretched, aiming to smother the startled cry forming on Gertrude's lips.

Gertrude's reflexes defied her age. As Billy lunged, her hand shot out, nails raking across his face with surprising ferocity. Searing pain exploded across his cheek.

"You little—" Billy snarled, momentarily stunned.

Gertrude's voice rang out, steely and defiant. "I'm not some helpless old lady, you bastard!"

She clawed at him again, blue eyes blazing with determination. Billy stumbled back, his carefully crafted plan unraveling. This wasn't how it was supposed to go. They always went quietly.

"Stop fighting!" he hissed, struggling to regain control.

Gertrude's mind raced. She knew she couldn't overpower him, not for long. But maybe...

"I've got more fight in me than you bargained for," she spat, buying time as an idea formed.

Billy lunged again, his face a mask of cold fury. This time, he managed to press the pillow against her face. Gertrude thrashed, her resistance weakening. Then, with a final, deliberate twitch, she went utterly still.

Her thoughts whirled. Play dead. It's your only chance. Don't breathe. Don't move a muscle.

Billy held the pillow for a few more seconds, then cautiously lifted it. Gertrude lay motionless, her eyes closed, chest barely moving.

"Damn," Billy muttered, his voice a mixture of relief and frustration. "Tougher than she looked."

Billy's eyes darted around the room, greed replacing the momentary panic. He wiped blood from the scratches on his face, wincing.

"Feisty old bat," he muttered, kicking off his methodical search.

He moved swiftly, yanking open drawers and rifling through their contents. A glint caught his eye – a pearl necklace nestled in a velvet box.

"Jackpot," Billy grinned, pocketing it.

His fingers brushed against an ornate brooch. "This'll fetch a nice price."

As he looted, Billy's thoughts raced. This job had gone sideways, but he could still salvage it. No witnesses, after all.

Gertrude lay motionless, every fiber of her being focused on maintaining the illusion. Her mind screamed to fight, to call for help, but she knew patience was her only weapon now.

Billy paused at a framed photo. "Sorry, granny. Nothing personal."

He slipped an antique watch into his pocket, its weight a comforting reminder of why he did this.

"One last sweep," Billy muttered, scanning the room.

Satisfied, he headed for the door. He cast a final glance at Gertrude's still form.

"Sweet dreams," he sneered, closing the door behind him.

The apartment fell silent, save for the pounding of Gertrude's heart, ready to spring into action.

The door clicked shut, and Gertrude's eyes flew open. She gasped, gulping air into her burning lungs. Her body trembled as she pushed herself up, adrenaline surging through her veins.

"You picked the wrong old lady, you bastard," she hissed, stumbling towards the phone.

Her fingers shook as she punched in 911, each ring an eternity.

"911, what's your emergency?"

"I've just been attacked," Gertrude said, her voice surprisingly steady. "He's still in the building. Send someone now."

She gripped the receiver tighter, her knuckles white. "Listen carefully. The man who attacked me is in his 30s, about 5'10", wearing a dirty baseball cap and jeans."

Gertrude's free hand touched her neck, phantom pressure lingering. "He has short brown hair, tried to pass himself off as maintenance. But here's the kicker – I got him good. There are deep scratches on his face."

Her blue eyes narrowed, a fierce determination blazing within them. "Make sure every cop in this city knows to look for those marks. I want this scumbag caught."

The dispatcher's voice crackled through the line. "Ma'am, are you hurt? Do you need medical assistance?"

Gertrude barked out a laugh. "Honey, I'm tougher than I look. Just get those officers here pronto. This old gal's got a score to settle."

A sharp knock at the door made Gertrude flinch. She approached cautiously, peering through the peephole. Relief washed over her at the sight of a badge.

"Mrs. Williams? Detective Jake Miller, NYPD," a deep voice called out.

Gertrude unlocked the door, coming face-to-face with a tall, broad-shouldered man. His dark eyes scanned the apartment before settling on her with concern.

"Are you alright, ma'am?" Jake asked, his tone gentle but authoritative.

Gertrude straightened her spine. "I've had better days, Detective, but I'm still kicking."

Jake nodded, pulling out a notepad. "Can you walk me through what happened?"

As Gertrude recounted the attack, Jake listened intently, his pen flying across the page. She didn't miss a detail, from Billy's initial friendly façade to the moment she felt his hands around her throat.

"And then," Gertrude said, a hint of pride in her voice, "I clawed that son of a gun's face like my life depended on it. Because it did."

Jake's eyebrows rose. "Smart move, Mrs. Williams. Those scratches will make him easier to identify."

Gertrude's lips thinned. "I hope they hurt like hell, too."

"Your quick thinking may have saved your life," Jake said, his admiration evident. "And it's given us a solid lead."

Gertrude felt a warmth in her chest, pushing back against the lingering fear. "Just doing what I had to, Detective. Now, what are you going to do to catch this creep?"

Jake's expression hardened. "Everything in our power, ma'am. Your description is already out to every officer in the city. We won't rest until he's behind bars."

"Good," Gertrude nodded, her blue eyes fierce. "Because neither will I."

Gertrude stood at her window, watching Detective Miller's broad shoulders disappear down the apartment hallway. Her hands trembled slightly, but her jaw was set with determination. She inhaled deeply, steadying herself.

"This isn't over, Billy," she muttered, her bright blue eyes narrowing. "Not by a long shot."

She turned from the window, surveying her apartment. The struggle had left visible marks—a toppled lamp, scattered cushions. Gertrude's gaze lingered on the pillow Billy had used to smother her. A chill ran down her spine, but she shook it off.

"Pull yourself together, old girl," she chided herself. "You've faced worse than this snake in the grass."

As she began tidying up, Gertrude's mind raced. "He thought he had me pegged," she thought. "Just another helpless old lady. Well, I showed him, didn't I?"

The phone rang, startling her. It was her neighbor, Martha.

"Gertie! I saw the police. Are you alright?" Martha's voice quavered with concern.

Gertrude sighed. "I'm fine, Martha. Just had a bit of excitement today. Nothing I couldn't handle."

"Should I come over? Do you need anything?"

"No, no," Gertrude insisted. "I'm right as rain. You stay put. I'll fill you in later."

As she hung up, Gertrude felt a surge of resolve. "That detective better do his job," she thought. "Because if he doesn't catch Billy, I just might have to do it myself."

Meanwhile, across town, Jake Miller hunched over his desk, case files spread before him. His eyes burned from fatigue, but he couldn't stop. Gertrude's description of Billy echoed in his mind.

"Got you now, you bastard," Jake muttered, piecing together the puzzle. The scratches, the maintenance worker disguise—it all fit a pattern he'd been tracking for months.

He grabbed his phone, punching in a number. "Johnson, get me everything we have on unsolved robberies targeting the elderly in the last year. And put out an APB on our suspect. We're bringing this guy down."

As Jake hung up, a grim smile played on his lips. The hunt was on, and Billy's days were numbered.

Chapter 9

Detective Jake Miller's phone buzzed, vibrating against his desk. He snatched it up, his heart rate quickening as he recognized the precinct's number.

"Miller," he barked into the receiver.

"Detective, we've got a match on Gertrude's attacker description."

Jake's fingers tightened around the phone. Finally, a break. "Send it over. I'm on my way."

He grabbed his jacket, mind racing. Could this be the lead they needed? The one that would crack the case wide open?

Officer Samantha Ortiz met him at the briefing room door, her dark eyes intense. "You hear about Gertrude's description?"

Jake nodded, pushing past her into the room. "Just got the call. Let's see what we've got."

They huddled over the desk, spreading out photos and reports. Jake's eyes darted from image to image, connecting dots, searching for patterns.

"Look here," Sam pointed to a grainy security camera still. "The build matches Gertrude's description perfectly."

Jake leaned in, squinting. "You're right. Same height, same broad shoulders."

His mind flashed to Gertrude's fierce blue eyes, her unwavering voice as she recounted the attack. She'd given them more than they'd hoped for.

"Pull up the files on our other elderly victims," Jake ordered, his voice tight with anticipation.

Sam complied, spreading out more photos and reports. "Jesus," she muttered. "The similarities are uncanny."

Jake's jaw clenched. "Same MO, same victim profile. We're dealing with a serial killer, Sam."

He paced the room, adrenaline coursing through his veins. We're close, he thought. So damn close to nailing this bastard.

"We need to cross-reference this description with known offenders," Jake said, turning back to Sam. "And put out an alert to all retirement communities in the area."

Sam nodded, already reaching for her phone. "On it, boss."

Jake stared at the evidence before him, determination etched into every line of his face. "We're going to catch this guy, Sam. Whatever it takes."

Jake ran a hand through his short-cropped hair, his mind racing. "The pattern's clear as day now. He's targeting elderly women, living alone."

Samantha nodded, her dark eyes scanning the reports. "And always in retirement communities. It's like he's shopping for victims."

"Exactly," Jake said, his voice tight with frustration. "He knows they're vulnerable, isolated. Easy targets."

Sam's brow furrowed. "But why suffocation? It's so... personal."

Jake's jaw clenched. "Control. He wants to see the life drain from their eyes. It's not just about the theft—he's getting off on the kill."

"Sick bastard," Sam muttered, then looked up sharply. "We need to warn these communities, Jake. Set up some kind of protective measure."

Jake nodded, already reaching for his phone. "I'll make some calls. We need to—"

The scene abruptly shifted.

Billy adjusted his faded baseball cap, eyes scanning the peaceful retirement community. His nondescript maintenance uniform blended seamlessly with the surroundings.

Perfect hunting ground, he thought, a small smile playing at the corners of his mouth.

He pushed his cart of tools down the sidewalk, nodding politely at passing residents. An old woman with a walker caught his eye—frail, alone. Billy's pulse quickened.

"Afternoon, ma'am," he called out cheerfully. "Just doing some routine checks. Everything alright with your plumbing?"

The woman smiled, unsuspecting. "Oh, it's fine, dear. But thank you for asking."

Billy nodded, moving on. Not today, he thought. But soon. He had all the time in the world, and the pickings here were ripe.

Jake's fingers flew over the keyboard, inputting the latest data points into the precinct's mapping software. The large screen on the wall flickered to life, displaying a constellation of red dots across the city grid.

"There," Samantha said, pointing to a cluster of markers. "Look at that concentration."

Jake leaned in, his eyes narrowing. "It's not random. He's moving in a pattern, Sam."

"Like a grid search," she murmured, her voice tight with realization. "He's methodically covering the area, block by block."

Jake's mind raced, connecting the dots. "If we extrapolate this pattern..." He traced a line with his finger, landing on an unmarked section of the map. "This could be his next target zone."

Samantha's jaw clenched. "We need to get units there, now."

"Hold on," Jake cautioned, his tone urgent but measured. "We can't tip him off. If he sees increased police presence, he might go to ground."

"So what's the play?" Samantha asked, her dark eyes locked on Jake's.

Jake ran a hand through his short-cropped hair, weighing their options. "We go in soft. Plainclothes officers, posing as new residents or visiting family members. Eyes and ears open, but nothing obvious."

Samantha nodded, already reaching for her phone. "I'll make the calls. We'll have people in place by nightfall."

As they moved to action, the scene shifted abruptly.

Billy knocked on the apartment door, his face a mask of friendly concern. "Maintenance," he called out, his voice pitched to be both audible and unthreatening. "Just need to check your pipes, ma'am."

The door opened, revealing Doris Lane, a frail woman in her eighties. "Oh, come in, dear. I wasn't expecting anyone."

Billy stepped inside, his practiced eye taking in the layout, the exits, the valuable trinkets adorning shelves. "Won't take but a minute, ma'am. You just go about your business."

As Doris turned away, Billy moved with startling speed. His arm wrapped around her throat, cutting off her cry before it could form. His other hand clamped over her mouth and nose, movements precise, almost mechanical.

There was no anger in his actions, no passion. Just the cold efficiency of a predator dispatching its prey. As Doris's struggles weakened, Billy's eyes remained flat, devoid of emotion. This was simply business, a means to an end.

And soon, it would be time to move on to the next target.

The phone on Jake's desk rang, its shrill tone cutting through the quiet hum of the precinct. He snatched it up, his free hand already reaching for a pen.

"Miller," he barked into the receiver. His face tightened as he listened, jotting down notes with quick, sharp strokes.

Samantha leaned forward, her eyes questioning. Jake held up a finger, his attention fixed on the call.

"Got it. We're on our way." He slammed the phone down, already on his feet. "Sam, we've got another one. Harold Perkins, 78. Found in his apartment off Maple Street."

Samantha's jaw clenched. "Fits the profile?"

"To a T. Let's move."

As they rushed out, Jake's mind raced. Another victim. The killer was escalating, getting bolder. We need to stop this bastard before he strikes again.

The scene shifted abruptly.

Billy emerged from Doris's apartment, his movements fluid and unhurried. He pulled the door shut behind him, the soft click of the lock barely audible. His hand slipped into his pocket, fingers curling around the weight of Doris's jewelry.

He strolled down the hallway, nodding politely to a passing resident. "All fixed up in there," he said with a friendly smile. "You folks have a good day now."

As he exited the building, Billy's eyes scanned the area, taking in every detail. No one paid him any attention. Just another maintenance worker finishing up his shift.

He allowed himself a small, satisfied smirk as he walked away. Another successful job. Another step closer to his goals. And still, no one suspected a thing.

Jake leaned forward, his elbows on the table, eyes intent on Gertrude Williams. The elderly woman sat straight-backed in her chair, her piercing blue gaze unflinching.

"Mrs. Williams, can you walk us through what happened again?" Jake asked, his tone gentle but urgent.

Gertrude's lips quirked in a wry smile. "Detective, my memory might be old, but it's not faulty. I've already told you everything."

Samantha interjected, her voice warm. "We appreciate that, Mrs. Williams. But sometimes, small details can make a big difference."

"Well," Gertrude sighed, "if you insist. He was about your height, Detective. Trim build, like he works out. Dark hair, neatly cut. But his eyes..." She paused, a shiver running through her. "Cold. Like a shark's."

Jake's pen scratched across his notepad. This matches our profile. He's meticulous, blends in. "Did he say anything specific?"

"Oh, he was all charm and smiles," Gertrude scoffed. "Until he wasn't. Said he was checking the smoke alarms. But I noticed his toolbelt was empty. That's when I knew something was off."

Samantha leaned in. "You're very observant, Mrs. Williams."

"When you get to my age, dear, you learn to pay attention."

The scene shifted abruptly.

Billy approached the quaint bungalow, his stride purposeful. He adjusted his cap, a friendly smile plastered on his face. Showtime.

He rang the doorbell, heart steady. The door opened, revealing Mildred Hawkins, her silver hair neatly coiffed.

"Good afternoon, ma'am," Billy said, voice warm and reassuring. "I'm here to check your water pressure. We've had some complaints in the area."

Mildred hesitated. "I don't recall any notice..."

Billy's smile widened. "Oh, it was rather last minute. But better safe than sorry, right?"

She wavered, then nodded. "I suppose so. Come in, then."

As Billy stepped inside, his eyes darted around, cataloging valuables. Easy mark. This won't take long.

"It'll just take a few minutes," he assured her, closing the door behind him.

Jake slapped a file onto the table, his jaw clenched. "Look at this, Sam. Five victims in three months, all elderly women living alone."

Samantha leaned in, her dark eyes scanning the documents. "The MO's consistent. Suffocation, jewelry stolen..." She paused, brow furrowing. "Wait, Jake. Look at the geographical spread."

Jake's eyes widened as he connected the dots. "He's moving systematically through the area. Damn it, we've got a serial on our hands."

"No doubt about it," Samantha agreed, her voice tight with determination. "We need to get ahead of this bastard before he strikes again."

Jake ran a hand through his hair, mind racing. "Gertrude's description is our best lead. Average height, nondescript clothing, but those eyes..."

"Cold. Predatory," Samantha finished. "We're dealing with a shark in human skin."

As they pieced together the evidence, Billy was already in Mildred's home, his friendly facade evaporating.

"I'm so sorry about this, Mrs. Hawkins," he said, voice dripping with false sincerity as he advanced on her trembling form.

Mildred's eyes widened in terror. "What are you—"

Billy moved with practiced efficiency, clamping a hand over her mouth. "Shh. It'll be over soon."

In moments, it was done. Billy pocketed Mildred's rings and necklace, his movements calm and precise. He surveyed the scene, satisfaction glinting in his cold eyes.

"Thanks for your hospitality," he murmured to Mildred's still form, then slipped out the door, blending seamlessly into the afternoon bustle.

Jake stood before Captain Reeves, his posture rigid with determination. Samantha flanked him, her eyes sharp and focused. The tension in the cramped office was palpable.

"Sir, we're convinced we're dealing with a serial killer targeting the elderly," Jake said, his voice tight with urgency. "The pattern is clear. We need to act now."

Captain Reeves leaned back, skepticism etched on his weathered face. "That's a bold claim, Miller. What evidence do you have?"

Samantha stepped forward, spreading crime scene photos across the desk. "The geographical pattern, sir. Each attack is methodical, moving through retirement communities in a clear progression."

Jake's mind raced, frustration building. We're running out of time. He forced his voice to remain steady. "The MO is consistent. Suffocation, stolen jewelry. And now we have a witness description."

"Gertrude Wilkins," Samantha interjected. "She gave us crucial details. Average height, nondescript clothing, but those eyes... cold, calculating."

Captain Reeves studied the evidence, his brow furrowed. Jake's heart pounded. Come on, see it. We need this.

"What are you proposing?" the captain finally asked.

Jake seized the opening. "Increased surveillance in retirement communities, sir. Undercover officers, security cameras. We're close to cracking this, I can feel it."

Samantha nodded emphatically. "We can't let another innocent person fall victim. We have to act now."

The captain's eyes narrowed, weighing their words. Jake held his breath, acutely aware of how much hinged on this moment.

Meanwhile, across town, Billy crouched in a dimly lit pawn shop backroom. His hands moved swiftly, sorting through Mildred's jewelry. Each piece held a memory of terror, a thrill he savored.

"Nice haul today," the pawnbroker grunted, eyeing the glittering pile.

Billy smiled, his face a mask of normalcy. "Just cleaning out my grandmother's old stuff," he lied smoothly. If only they knew how close I was. The danger, the thrill of it all.

As he pocketed the cash, a news report flickered on a nearby TV. "Police urge caution as suspicious deaths in retirement communities continue to—"

Billy's pulse quickened, a mix of excitement and wariness coursing through him. They're getting closer. But they'll never catch me. I'm too smart, too careful.

He stepped out into the fading daylight, already planning his next move. The game was far from over.

Chapter 10

Billy Thompson adjusted his worn baseball cap and plastered on a friendly smile as he approached Mary Simmons' door. His heart raced with anticipation, but his outward demeanor remained calm and unassuming. He'd done this before. The maintenance worker act was foolproof.

He raised his hand and knocked firmly. Three sharp raps.

The door creaked open, revealing Mary's gentle face framed by wispy gray hair. Her brown eyes widened slightly as she took in Billy's appearance.

"Good afternoon, ma'am," Billy said, his voice warm and reassuring. "I'm here to check on that leaky faucet you reported."

Mary hesitated, her brow furrowing. "I'm sorry, I don't recall..."

Billy's mind raced. He couldn't lose his chance now. "Management sent me over as a precaution. There've been some plumbing issues in the building lately."

Mary's shoulders relaxed slightly, but wariness still tinged her voice. "Oh, I see. Well, I suppose it wouldn't hurt to take a look."

She stepped back, allowing Billy to enter. He fought to keep his excitement in check as he crossed the threshold. Another mark, another opportunity.

"Kitchen's this way," Mary said softly, leading him through the tidy living room.

Billy's eyes darted around, cataloging valuables. A silver picture frame. An antique clock. Potential targets.

"So, how long have you lived here, Mrs...?" Billy asked, maintaining his friendly facade.

"Simmons. Mary Simmons," she replied. "Going on fifteen years now."

Billy nodded, his mind already plotting his next move. The gentle soul before him had no idea of the danger that had just walked through her door.

As Mary turned her back to lead Billy into the kitchen, his demeanor shifted. The friendly mask slipped away, replaced by a cold, calculating stare. In one swift motion, he lunged forward, hands outstretched towards Mary's frail form.

"What are you—" Mary's words cut off as she spun around, her eyes widening in shock.

To Billy's surprise, Mary's fragile appearance belied an unexpected strength. She ducked, narrowly avoiding his grasp, and stumbled backwards. Her hand shot out, grasping the edge of the kitchen counter for support.

"Get out!" Mary's voice, though shaky, carried a steely resolve that caught Billy off guard.

He hesitated for a split second, thrown by her defiance. "Now, now, let's not make this difficult," he growled, advancing again.

Mary's eyes darted around the kitchen, searching for anything she could use to defend herself. Her fingers closed around a heavy ceramic mug on the counter.

As Billy reached for her, Mary swung the mug with surprising force. It connected with his temple, causing him to stagger backwards.

"Damn it!" Billy hissed, touching the spot where the mug had struck. His fingers came away with a smear of blood.

Mary's chest heaved with exertion, but her gaze remained steady. "I've lived through worse than you," she said, her voice low but firm. "You picked the wrong house, young man."

Billy's mind raced. This wasn't going according to plan. How could this frail old woman be giving him so much trouble? He needed to regain control of the situation, fast.

Mary's heart pounded as she edged toward the living room, her eyes never leaving Billy. The phone. She had to reach the phone. Her fingers trembled as she inched closer to the side table.

"Don't even think about it," Billy snarled, lunging forward.

Mary ducked, her arthritic joints screaming in protest. She snatched the cordless phone, her shaky hands fumbling with the buttons. 9-1-1. Simple. Direct. She'd practiced this.

Billy's footsteps thundered behind her. Mary's thumb hit 'call' just as his fingers grazed her shoulder.

"911, what's your emergency?" The operator's voice was clear, steady.

"Help," Mary managed, her own voice surprisingly calm despite the chaos. "There's a man in my house. He's attacking me." She rattled off her address, muscle memory from years of giving directions to concerned relatives.

Billy's face contorted with rage. "Hang up!"

Mary's mind raced. Keep talking. Keep the line open. "He's here now. I'm at 1852 Maple—"

The phone clattered to the floor as Billy's hand clamped over her mouth. But Mary had done it. Help was coming.

Sirens wailed in the distance, growing louder with each passing second. Billy's grip loosened, panic flashing across his face.

"No, no, no," he muttered, backing away.

Mary sagged against the wall, relief washing over her. She'd done it. She'd survived.

The front door burst open, a whirlwind of uniforms and urgent voices filling the space. Paramedics rushed to Mary's side, their faces etched with concern.

"Ma'am, are you alright?" A young woman in an EMT uniform knelt beside her, checking her vitals.

Mary nodded, wincing as the adrenaline faded and pain set in. "I'm okay," she said softly. "Just a bit shaken up."

As the paramedics tended to her injuries, Mary's gaze drifted to the shattered mug on the kitchen floor. A small smile tugged at her lips. Who would have thought her favorite tea mug would end up saving her life?

The gravity of the situation settled over her like a heavy blanket. She'd come so close to becoming another statistic, another victim. But she'd fought back. She'd survived.

Mary closed her eyes, letting out a shaky breath. The nightmare was over, but the memory would linger. She knew she'd need time to heal, not just physically, but emotionally. But for now, she was alive. And that was enough.

Detective Jake Miller strode into the hospital room, his tall frame filling the doorway. His sharp eyes scanned the scene, taking in every detail before settling on Mary.

"Mrs. Simmons?" he asked, his deep voice softened with concern. "I'm Detective Miller. How are you holding up?"

Mary looked up from her hospital bed, her kind brown eyes meeting Jake's. "I'm alright, Detective. A bit sore, but I'll manage."

Jake pulled up a chair, leaning in. "I know this is difficult, but can you tell me what happened?"

Mary nodded, her voice steady despite her ordeal. "He came to the door, said he was from maintenance. I should've known better, but he seemed so friendly..."

As Mary recounted the attack, Jake listened intently, his brow furrowing. Something about her description tickled at his memory.

"Can you describe him for me?" Jake asked, pen poised over his notepad.

Mary's eyes closed, concentrating. "Tall, lean. Dark hair, a bit shaggy. But his eyes... cold, almost predatory. And a scar, right here." She touched her left cheek.

Jake's pen froze mid-sentence. The description matched Gertrude's account perfectly. His pulse quickened as pieces began falling into place.

"Mrs. Simmons, you've been incredibly brave," Jake said, squeezing her hand gently. "We're going to catch this guy, I promise you that."

As he left the room, Jake's mind raced. Two attacks, same M.O., same description. This wasn't just a random assault. They were dealing with a serial predator, and time was running out.

Jake's jaw clenched as he strode down the hospital corridor, his mind churning. The trespassing incident from months ago flashed vividly in his memory. He'd dismissed it then—a minor offense, a slap on the wrist. Now it felt like a missed opportunity, a chance to have stopped this monster before he escalated.

"Damn it," he muttered, running a hand through his cropped hair. "We had him. We had him right there."

His phone buzzed. Jake glanced at the screen, a spark of hope igniting as he saw the name.

"Ortiz," he answered, his voice taut with urgency. "Tell me you've got something."

"I might," came Samantha's crisp reply. "Just pulled up to the hospital. Where are you?"

Jake's pace quickened. "Third floor, heading to the elevator. Meet me in the lobby."

Moments later, the elevator doors slid open, revealing Samantha's focused expression. She held a thick file folder, her dark ponytail swinging as she fell into step beside Jake.

"You look like you've seen a ghost, Miller," she said, her keen eyes scanning his face. "What's going on?"

Jake's voice was low, intense. "I think we've got our guy, Sam. The description matches perfectly with—"

"The trespassing case from last spring," Samantha finished, already flipping open the folder. "I had the same hunch. That's why I grabbed these records."

Jake felt a surge of gratitude for his partner's intuition. "You're a lifesaver, Ortiz. Let's find somewhere quiet to go through these."

As they headed for an empty conference room, Jake's determination solidified. They were close—he could feel it. And this time, he wouldn't let the bastard slip away.

Jake and Samantha hunched over the scattered files, their eyes darting across pages of reports and witness statements. The conference room hummed with their focused energy.

"Look here," Samantha pointed, her finger tracing a line. "The M.O. matches. Posing as maintenance, targeting elderly women living alone."

Jake nodded, his jaw clenched. "And the physical description is spot on. But we need something concrete, a name, a—"

His words cut off as he flipped to the next page. There, staring back at him, was a mugshot that made his blood run cold. A man with unkempt brown hair peeking from under a stained baseball cap, eyes holding a calculated friendliness that now seemed sinister.

"Son of a bitch," Jake breathed, triumph and urgency surging through him. "That's him. William Thompson."

Samantha leaned in, her eyes widening. "Billy Thompson? The guy from the trespassing case?"

Jake's mind raced, pieces clicking into place. "It all fits. The charm, the way he blends in. How did we miss this?"

"We didn't have the full picture then," Samantha said, her voice tight with determination. "But we do now."

Jake stood abruptly, adrenaline coursing through him. "We've got to move fast. He knows we're onto him after Mary's attack. He'll be looking to run or find another victim."

Samantha was already on her feet, gathering the files. "I'll put out an APB and alert all units. Where do you want to start?"

Jake's eyes narrowed, his focus laser-sharp. "His last known address. It's a long shot, but it's all we've got. Let's go."

As they rushed out, Jake's mind whirled with possibilities. They had a name, a face. The hunt was on, and this time, Jake wouldn't rest until William Thompson was behind bars.

Jake's jaw clenched as he strode down the hospital corridor, his footsteps echoing with purpose. "We're not letting this bastard slip away," he growled, more to himself than to Samantha.

"Jake," Samantha called, matching his pace. "What's our next move after checking his address?"

He paused, turning to face her. "We'll need to dig deeper. Employment records, known associates, any pattern to his movements."

Jake's mind raced, piecing together the puzzle. "This guy, he's smart. Blends in, probably changes jobs frequently. We need to think like him."

Samantha nodded, her expression mirroring his determination. "I'll get the tech team on it, see if we can track any digital footprint."

"Good," Jake said, resuming his stride. "And we need to warn potential targets. Retirement communities, assisted living facilities. Anywhere he might find vulnerable victims."

As they pushed through the hospital doors, the cool night air hit Jake's face. He took a deep breath, steeling himself for the chase ahead.

"You know," he said, turning to Samantha as they approached their car, "guys like Thompson, they get cocky. Think they're invincible. That's when they make mistakes."

Samantha raised an eyebrow. "You think he'll slip up?"

Jake's eyes hardened. "I'm counting on it. And when he does, we'll be there."

As he slid into the driver's seat, Jake felt a familiar surge of determination. The hunt was on, and William Thompson's days of freedom were numbered.

Chapter 11

The courtroom door creaked open. Billy Thompson shuffled in, handcuffed and flanked by guards. His eyes darted around, taking in every detail.

Hushed whispers filled the air. "That's him," someone murmured. "The monster."

Billy suppressed a smirk. If only they knew the half of it.

Judge Harriet Stone's gavel cracked like a gunshot. "Order in the court. The trial of William Thompson will now commence."

Billy's gaze swept over the gallery, lingering on the victims' families. Grief etched deep lines in their faces. Anger smoldered in their eyes. A woman in the front row clutched a framed photo, her knuckles white.

Fools. They had no idea what they were dealing with.

"All rise for the Honorable Judge Stone," the bailiff announced.

As the crowd stood, Billy caught sight of his brother Frank in the back. Frank's jaw was clenched, his massive frame tense. Their eyes met briefly. Frank looked away first.

Traitor, Billy thought. You're supposed to have my back.

Judge Stone's stern voice cut through his thoughts. "Be seated. Mr. Thompson, you stand accused of multiple counts of theft, fraud, and murder. How do you plead?"

Billy straightened, adopting an expression of bewildered innocence. "Not guilty, Your Honor."

A collective gasp rippled through the courtroom. The photo-clutching woman let out a strangled sob.

Stay cool, Billy reminded himself. You've got this under control. They've got nothing solid on you.

As the proceedings continued, Billy tuned out the droning voices. His mind raced, analyzing every angle, every potential weakness in the prosecution's case. He'd prepared for this. Studied law books in prison. He knew how to play the system.

A flicker of movement caught his eye. Frank shifting uncomfortably in his seat.

Poor Frank, Billy mused. Always the dutiful one. Wonder how it feels knowing your own flesh and blood is capable of such things?

But capability and guilt were two very different matters. Billy allowed himself a small, secret smile.

Let the games begin.

District Attorney Sarah Hawkins rose from her seat, her posture ramrod straight as she approached the jury. Her eyes, sharp and unyielding, swept across the twelve faces before her.

"Ladies and gentlemen of the jury," she began, her voice cutting through the tense silence, "the man sitting before you is not just a thief. He is a predator."

Billy's jaw clenched imperceptibly. Predator? That's a bit dramatic.

"William Thompson systematically targeted our community's most vulnerable members," Hawkins continued. "The elderly. The infirm. Those who trusted him with their care and their lives."

She's good, Billy admitted grudgingly. But I'm better.

"We will prove, beyond any shadow of doubt, that Mr. Thompson's actions were not just criminal, but monstrous. Six lives lost. Millions in stolen assets. Families shattered."

The DA's words hung heavy in the air. Billy forced himself to maintain a neutral expression, even as he felt the weight of the gallery's stares boring into his back.

As Hawkins concluded her opening statement, Judge Stone called the first witness.

"The prosecution calls Detective Jacob Miller to the stand."

Jake stood, his broad shoulders set with determination as he strode to the witness box. As he was sworn in, his eyes briefly met Billy's. There was no hatred there, just a steely resolve that made Billy's skin crawl.

This guy's gonna be trouble.

"Detective Miller," Hawkins began, "can you walk us through the evidence that led to Mr. Thompson's arrest?"

Jake nodded, his voice steady. "We recovered surveillance footage from three separate crime scenes showing a man matching the defendant's description entering the victims' homes."

Billy's mind raced. Impossible. I was careful.

"Additionally," Jake continued, "forensic analysis of the defendant's computer revealed detailed financial records of the victims, including account numbers and passwords that were later used to drain their assets."

Damn it, Frank, Billy thought bitterly. You were supposed to wipe that hard drive.

As Jake methodically laid out the case against him, Billy felt a bead of sweat form on his brow. For the first time since his arrest, a flicker of doubt crept into his mind.

Maybe I've underestimated these people after all.

Samantha Ortiz stepped up to the witness stand, her dark ponytail swinging with purpose. As she was sworn in, her sharp eyes scanned the courtroom, lingering briefly on Billy Thompson's impassive face.

"Officer Ortiz," the DA began, "can you describe your role in this investigation?"

Sam's voice rang clear and confident. "I was the lead investigator on the cyber forensics team. We analyzed the digital footprint left by the perpetrator."

She leaned forward, her tone unwavering. "We uncovered a sophisticated network of shell companies and offshore accounts used to launder the stolen funds. Each transaction was meticulously planned and executed."

Billy's jaw clenched. How the hell did they trace that?

"And were you able to link these transactions to the defendant?" the DA pressed.

"Absolutely," Sam replied, her eyes flashing with conviction. "We found a series of encrypted messages on Mr. Thompson's devices that detailed the transfers. The timestamps aligned perfectly with the victims' accounts being drained."

As Sam continued her testimony, her dedication to the case was palpable. She spoke with a quiet intensity, determined to give voice to those who'd been silenced.

When Sam finished, the courtroom buzzed with tension. The next witness was called.

"The prosecution calls Gertrude Williams to the stand."

A hush fell over the room as Gertrude rose, her white hair gleaming under the fluorescent lights. She walked with measured steps, her chin held high.

As she settled into the witness box, her bright blue eyes locked onto Billy. There was no fear in her gaze, only fierce determination.

"Mrs. Williams," the DA began gently, "can you tell us about your encounter with the defendant?"

Gertrude's voice was clear and steady. "He came to my home, posing as a financial advisor. But I've been around long enough to spot a wolf in sheep's clothing."

Gertrude's words hung in the air, electric. The jury leaned forward, captivated by her unwavering gaze and the strength in her voice.

"He tried to charm me, but I saw right through it," Gertrude continued, her eyes narrowing. "When I refused to sign anything, his mask slipped. The look in his eyes..." She paused, a shiver running through her. "I knew I was in danger."

Billy shifted in his seat, his face a careful blank.

Gertrude's chin lifted. "But I wasn't about to become another victim. I fought back."

A collective gasp rippled through the courtroom.

"You fought back?" the DA prompted.

"Damn right I did," Gertrude said, a hint of pride in her voice. "I may be old, but I'm not helpless. I grabbed my cane and swung for the fences."

Several jurors exchanged impressed glances.

"Mrs. Williams," the DA said, "your bravery is commendable. What happened next?"

"He ran," Gertrude said simply. "And I called the police."

As Gertrude finished her testimony, the atmosphere in the courtroom was charged. The DA thanked her, and she stepped down, her eyes meeting those of the other victims' families in solidarity.

The judge called a brief recess. When court resumed, a new witness took the stand.

"The prosecution calls Mary Simmons."

Mary approached slowly, her gentle demeanor a stark contrast to Gertrude's fiery presence. As she settled into the witness box, her eyes briefly met Billy's. He looked away first.

"Mrs. Simmons," the DA began softly, "can you tell us about your experience with the defendant?"

Mary took a deep breath, her hands clasped tightly in her lap. "He came to our retirement community often," she said, her voice quiet but steady. "Always so helpful, so charming. We had no reason to suspect..."

Her voice trailed off, and she closed her eyes for a moment, gathering strength.

"What did you notice, Mrs. Simmons?" the DA prompted gently.

Mary's eyes opened, a quiet determination shining in them. "Little things at first. Items missing from apartments. Then larger sums of money vanishing from accounts. I started keeping notes, watching more closely."

Billy's fingers twitched, his carefully constructed facade beginning to crack.

Billy's court-appointed lawyer, a wiry man with thinning hair, rose from his seat. His eyes darted nervously around the courtroom as he cleared his throat.

"Your Honor, the defense would like to present evidence of Mr. Thompson's mental instability," he began, his voice wavering slightly.

Billy's jaw clenched, his gaze fixed on the floor.

The lawyer fumbled with some papers. "We have records indicating Mr. Thompson suffered a traumatic brain injury in his youth, which may have impaired his judgment and—"

"Objection!" The DA's voice cut through the air. "This is the first we're hearing of any such injury. Where's the documentation?"

The judge peered over his glasses. "Counselor?"

Billy's lawyer swallowed hard. "We're... still locating the medical records, Your Honor."

A murmur rippled through the courtroom. Billy's fingers drummed silently on the table, his face a mask of forced calm.

The judge frowned. "Overruled. Continue, but tread carefully."

As the defense stumbled through a weak argument about diminished capacity, Billy's mind raced. This isn't working. They don't understand. I had to do it. They were wasting their money, their lives...

The DA stood, her eyes blazing. "Your Honor, the prosecution would like to rebut this baseless claim."

She strode to the center of the courtroom, her presence commanding attention. "The evidence shows Mr. Thompson's actions were anything but impaired. They were calculated, meticulous, and chillingly deliberate."

Billy's pulse quickened. She doesn't know the half of it.

"Bank records show systematic transfers," the DA continued, her voice sharp. "Surveillance footage captures him methodically casing multiple retirement communities. This was no impulsive act, but a carefully orchestrated series of crimes."

Billy's lips twitched into the ghost of a smile. She's good. But she still doesn't get it. I was helping them, in a way. They just can't see it yet.

The DA's voice grew colder. "Mr. Thompson preyed on the vulnerable with precision and forethought. Mental instability? No. This is the work of a cold, calculating criminal who knew exactly what he was doing."

As she spoke, Billy's mask of indifference began to slip, revealing a glimmer of the ruthless intelligence beneath.

The district attorney's voice rang out, clear and resolute, as she delivered her closing argument. "Ladies and gentlemen of the jury, we've seen overwhelming evidence of William Thompson's guilt."

Billy's eyes narrowed, watching her every move. She's building to something. I can feel it.

"This man," she continued, gesturing towards Billy, "meticulously planned and executed a series of heinous crimes against our most vulnerable citizens. Not out of desperation or misguided altruism, but out of pure, unbridled greed."

The jury leaned forward, captivated. Billy's jaw clenched. They're hanging on her every word.

"Mr. Thompson didn't just steal money. He stole trust, dignity, and in some cases, lives." Her voice cracked with emotion. "Remember Gertrude Williams' testimony. Remember Mary Simmons' quiet strength. These are the lives he nearly destroyed."

Billy's fingers twitched, itching to object, to explain. They don't understand. I was setting them free from their mundane existences.

"The defense would have you believe Mr. Thompson was not in his right mind. But the evidence tells a different story. A story of careful planning, of manipulation, of a predator selecting his prey."

The DA's eyes locked with each juror in turn. "You have the power to deliver justice. To show that we, as a society, protect our elders. I urge you to find William Thompson guilty on all counts."

As she returned to her seat, a heavy silence fell over the courtroom. The judge addressed the jury, "You may now retire to deliberate."

The scraping of chairs filled the air as the jury filed out. Billy's gaze followed them, his mind racing. What are they thinking? Can they see through the DA's emotional appeal?

In the gallery, victims' families clasped hands, their faces etched with anxiety. The prosecution team exchanged tense glances, years of work hanging in the balance.

Billy sat motionless, his outward calm belying the storm within. This is it. My fate in their hands. But they don't know the whole story. They never will.

The courtroom door clicked shut behind the last juror, sealing off the deliberation room. A collective exhale seemed to ripple through the gallery, followed by an oppressive silence.

Billy's eyes darted to his brother Frank, searching for any sign of support. Frank's jaw was clenched, his gaze fixed on the empty jury box. The disappointment radiating from him was palpable.

"All rise," the bailiff's voice cut through the quiet.

As chairs scraped against the floor, Billy stood, his legs unsteady. The judge's words barely registered as he dismissed the court until the jury reached a verdict.

People began to file out, their hushed whispers a stark contrast to the earlier tension. Billy turned to his lawyer. "How long do you think—"

"Impossible to say," his attorney cut him off, already packing his briefcase. "Could be hours. Could be days."

As the courtroom emptied, Billy caught sight of Gertrude Williams. She stood ramrod straight, her blue eyes piercing as they met his. A chill ran down his spine.

She knows. She sees right through me.

Gertrude's lips curved into a thin smile, more a show of determination than mirth. "Justice comes for us all, Mr. Thompson," she said, her voice carrying clearly across the room. "One way or another."

Billy swallowed hard, fighting to maintain his composure. I'm not done yet. This isn't over.

But as the bailiff led him away, doubt gnawed at the edges of his confidence. The weight of uncertainty pressed down, leaving him—and everyone else—in suspense, awaiting the jury's decision that would determine his fate.

Chapter 12

The courtroom doors swung open with a heavy thud. Twelve men and women filed in, their faces etched with the weight of their decision. The air crackled with tension, electric and suffocating.

Judge Harriet Martinez's gavel cut through the silence. "Has the jury reached a verdict?"

The foreperson, a middle-aged woman with graying hair, rose slowly. Her hands trembled slightly as she unfolded a small piece of paper. The entire room seemed to lean forward, collectively holding its breath.

"We have, Your Honor."

The judge nodded. "Please state your verdict."

The foreperson's voice rang out, clear and steady despite the gravity of the moment. "On all counts, we find the defendant, William 'Billy' Thompson, guilty."

A wave of muted reactions rippled through the courtroom. Gasps of relief mingled with quiet sobs. Someone whispered, "Thank God." Another muttered, "It's over."

From the gallery, an elderly woman clutched her chest, tears streaming down her wrinkled cheeks. A young man next to her wrapped an arm around her shoulders, his jaw clenched tight.

The judge's voice cut through the murmurs. "Order in the court."

As the noise settled, the air remained thick with emotion—relief, sorrow, and a grim sense of justice served. The verdict hung over the room like a heavy cloud, its implications settling into the minds of all present.

Billy Thompson sat motionless at the defense table, his trademark baseball cap absent, revealing his unkempt brown hair. His face remained impassive, a mask of indifference that belied the gravity of his situation.

The judge's voice broke the momentary silence. "The court thanks the jury for their service. You are dismissed."

As the jurors filed out, their shoulders seemed lighter, unburdened by the weight of their decision. The courtroom buzzed with subdued conversation, the tension of the past weeks finally finding release in hushed whispers and quiet embraces.

Billy's eyes darted around the courtroom, his practiced calm wavering for a split second. He tugged at his collar, a bead of sweat forming on his temple. "Keep it together," he muttered under his breath, forcing his features back into a mask of nonchalance.

His fingers twitched, itching to adjust the baseball cap that wasn't there. He'd spent years perfecting his unassuming demeanor, and now, stripped of his usual props, he felt exposed. Billy leaned towards his lawyer, whispering, "Can we appeal? There's gotta be something we can do."

The lawyer shook his head imperceptibly, his lips a tight line.

Billy's mind raced. He'd talked his way out of tighter spots before. Maybe if he could catch the judge's eye, show some remorse... He cleared his throat, preparing to speak.

But the judge's gavel cracked through the air, silencing the room. Judge Harriet Simmons, her silver hair pulled back in a severe bun, peered over her glasses at the courtroom. She took a deep breath, her weathered face etched with the weight of what was to come.

"William Thompson," she began, her voice low and resonant. "The crimes you have committed against our community's most vulnerable members are unconscionable."

Billy's jaw clenched. He'd heard that tone before – from social workers, teachers, bosses. Always underestimating him. He fought the urge to smirk. If they only knew how smart he really was...

Judge Simmons continued, her words measured and heavy. "You preyed upon those who trusted you, those who welcomed you into their homes and lives."

A ripple of anger passed through the gallery. Billy resisted the urge to turn and look. Instead, he fixed his gaze on the judge, his expression a carefully crafted blend of regret and humility.

Judge Simmons leaned forward, her eyes piercing through Billy's facade. "For each of the seven counts of first-degree murder, you are hereby sentenced to life in prison without the possibility of parole. These sentences are to be served consecutively."

The words hit Billy like a physical blow. His carefully constructed mask slipped for a moment, revealing a flash of panic in his eyes.

"Furthermore," the judge continued, her voice gaining strength, "for the additional charges of theft, fraud, and elder abuse, you are sentenced to an additional 50 years. Mr. Thompson, you will spend the rest of your natural life behind bars."

The finality of her words echoed through the courtroom. Billy's mind raced. This couldn't be happening. There had to be a way out.

As two officers approached to lead him away, Billy made his move. He turned towards the judge, his face transforming into a mask of remorse.

"Your Honor, please," he said, his voice cracking with practiced emotion. "I... I never meant for anyone to get hurt. If you could just—"

"That's enough, Mr. Thompson," Judge Simmons cut him off sharply. "Officers, remove the defendant."

As the officers gripped his arms, Billy's desperation grew. He scanned the courtroom, searching for a sympathetic face. His gaze landed on an elderly woman in the gallery.

"Ma'am," he called out, his voice taking on the gentle tone he'd used to gain trust in the retirement communities. "You understand, don't you? It was all just a misunderstanding..."

But his words fell on deaf ears as he was led towards the exit. Billy's mind raced, trying to formulate a new plan. This couldn't be the end. He'd find a way out. He always did.

Jake Miller's eyes locked with Samantha Ortiz's across the courtroom. A silent understanding passed between them, years of shared cases and late nights distilled into a single glance.

"We got him," Jake mouthed, his jaw clenched.

Sam nodded, her ponytail bobbing slightly. "Finally," she whispered back.

Jake felt a grim satisfaction settle in his chest. He leaned towards Sam, keeping his voice low. "Remember that first interview with Gertrude?"

"How could I forget?" Sam's lips quirked. "She saw right through his act."

"Damn right she did," Jake agreed, his eyes drifting to where Gertrude sat with Mary. "Without her..."

"We wouldn't be here," Sam finished.

Jake watched the two elderly women, their hands clasped tightly. Gertrude's bright blue eyes were steely, her posture rigid. Mary, beside her, dabbed at her eyes with a tissue.

"You okay?" Jake heard Mary ask softly.

Gertrude's response was barely audible. "I will be."

Jake felt a lump form in his throat. How many lives had Billy Thompson destroyed? How many families torn apart?

"We did good, Sam," he murmured, his voice rough. "But it doesn't bring them back."

Sam's hand found his shoulder, squeezing gently. "No," she agreed. "But it's something."

Jake nodded, his eyes still on Gertrude and Mary. They'd weathered this storm together, these two survivors. He hoped they'd find some peace now.

"Come on," Sam said, rising. "Let's go thank them."

Jake stood, straightening his tie. It was over, but the weight of it all still pressed down on him. As they approached Gertrude and Mary, he took a deep breath. There was still work to be done.

Gertrude's voice was soft but unwavering as she turned to Mary. "We made it through, dear. Just like we said we would."

Mary's hand trembled in Gertrude's grasp. "I don't know if I could've done it without you, Gert."

"Nonsense," Gertrude replied, her blue eyes sparkling with a mix of determination and warmth. "You're stronger than you think. We both are."

She patted Mary's hand, her touch gentle yet reassuring. "Remember what we talked about? This is just the beginning of our healing."

Mary nodded, a ghost of a smile crossing her lips. "You're right. It's just... hard to believe it's over."

"Oh, I know," Gertrude said, her voice taking on a hint of her usual feistiness. "But we showed that monster, didn't we? He thought he could break us, but here we are."

Mary's smile grew a little stronger. "Here we are," she echoed.

Across the courtroom, Evelyn Davis sat alone, her posture rigid and her gaze distant. Her mind raced with possibilities and plans, each thought tinged with a fierce protectiveness.

"Never again," she muttered under her breath, her fingers drumming against her knee. "I won't let this happen again."

She glanced around the emptying courtroom, her eyes narrowing. "We need better screening processes," she thought. "Stricter background checks. Maybe even security cameras in common areas."

The weight of responsibility settled heavily on her shoulders. She'd trusted Billy, they all had. That trust had cost lives.

"I'll talk to the board tomorrow," Evelyn decided, her jaw set with determination. "We'll make changes. Whatever it takes to keep our residents safe."

As she stood to leave, her gaze fell on Gertrude and Mary. A pang of guilt shot through her, but it was quickly replaced by resolve.

"I owe it to them," she thought. "To all of them. To do better."

Evelyn's blue eyes flashed with determination as she pulled out her phone, fingers flying over the screen. "Security upgrades... staff vetting... emergency protocols," she murmured, creating a detailed list. Her brow furrowed in concentration, each item a shield against future harm.

She glanced up, catching sight of a young woman clutching a framed photo. The woman's eyes were red-rimmed, but there was a glimmer of peace in her expression. Beside her, an older couple held hands tightly, their faces etched with both sorrow and relief.

"Mr. Grayson's daughter," Evelyn thought, recognizing the photo. "And the Millers. They lost their aunt."

She swallowed hard, her throat tight. "I failed them once," she thought. "Never again."

Evelyn stood, smoothing her blazer. She approached the families, her steps measured but purposeful.

"I know words can't undo what's been done," she began softly, "but I want you to know we're taking every measure to ensure this never happens again."

The young woman looked up, her grip on the photo loosening slightly. "You mean that?" she asked, her voice barely above a whisper.

Evelyn nodded, her expression resolute. "With everything I have," she promised. "Your loved ones deserved better, and I swear to you, we will do better."

As she spoke, Evelyn felt the weight of her commitment settle over her like armor. The path ahead would be challenging, but she was ready. For the victims, for their families, and for every resident who trusted her, she would build a fortress of safety and care.

The young woman nodded, a tear slipping down her cheek as she clutched the photo to her chest. "Thank you," she whispered, her voice breaking.

Across the room, Gertrude Williams watched the exchange, her bright blue eyes sharp with understanding. She turned to Mary, squeezing her hand.

"It's over," Gertrude said, her voice low but steady. "That monster can't hurt anyone else now."

Mary's shoulders shook as she leaned into Gertrude. "I keep thinking about Sarah," she murmured. "And all the others."

Gertrude's jaw tightened. "We honor them by living, Mary. By making sure this never happens again."

As the courtroom began to empty, the air felt lighter, as if a great weight had been lifted. Families embraced, some crying softly, others offering quiet words of comfort. A father knelt by his young son, explaining in hushed tones that the bad man was going away for a long time.

Jake caught Samantha's eye across the room, a silent acknowledgment passing between them. They'd done it. Justice had been served, but the cost had been high.

As the last of the spectators filed out, the empty courtroom seemed to hold its breath. The echo of the gavel still lingered, a final punctuation to the chapter that had consumed so many lives.

Gertrude was the last to leave, her steps slow but purposeful. She paused at the doorway, looking back at the now-silent room.

"It's not enough," she thought, her heart heavy. "But it's a start."

With that, she stepped into the hallway, leaving behind the ghosts of what had been and facing the challenges of what was yet to come.

Chapter 13

The clock ticked softly in the dim office. Jake's knuckles whitened as he gripped his knees, avoiding the therapist's steady gaze. Muted traffic sounds filtered through the window.

"Detective Miller, can you walk me through what happened?"

Jake's jaw clenched. The words stuck in his throat. How could he possibly convey the weight of it all? The victims' faces flashed through his mind - elderly, vulnerable, betrayed.

"It started with a routine welfare check," he began haltingly. "We had no idea what we were walking into."

Jake's eyes darted to the door. Part of him wanted to bolt, to escape reliving it all. But he forced himself to continue.

"The smell hit us first. That sickly sweet odor of decay."

His stomach churned at the memory. Jake swallowed hard.

"We found her there, abandoned. Left to die alone."

The therapist nodded encouragingly. "And how did that make you feel?"

Rage and helplessness warred inside Jake. "Like I'd failed her. Failed all of them."

He exhaled sharply, struggling to maintain composure. "We're supposed to protect people. But we were always two steps behind."

Jake's fists tightened. "Billy Evans. That monster was out there for months, preying on the defenseless. And we couldn't stop him."

The silence stretched as Jake battled his emotions. Finally, he looked up, eyes haunted.

"How do I move past this?" he asked hoarsely. "How do I forget their faces?"

***

Across town, Samantha perched on the edge of a leather couch, spine rigid. Her counselor leaned forward, concern etched on her face.

"The nightmares are getting worse," Sam admitted, voice low. "I see them every time I close my eyes. The victims, staring at me. Accusing me."

She shuddered, recalling last night's vivid dream. "They ask why I didn't save them. Why I let them suffer."

Sam's eyes blazed with determination. "But I won't let their deaths be in vain. I can't change the past, but I can damn well work to prevent it from happening again."

Her counselor nodded. "That's a noble goal, Samantha. But how do you plan to balance that drive with your own mental health?"

Sam's laugh was bitter. "Balance? There's no balance when monsters are out there. I'll sleep when I know our community is safe."

She stood abruptly, pacing the small office. "I've started volunteering at the senior center. Teaching self-defense classes. It's not enough, but it's something."

Sam's voice softened. "I owe it to them. To all the victims we couldn't save. I have to make this right."

The community center buzzed with nervous energy as Gertrude Williams took her place behind the podium. Her white hair gleamed under the fluorescent lights, her bright blue eyes scanning the crowd with sharp intelligence. She gripped the edges of the lectern, her knuckles whitening slightly.

"Good evening, everyone," Gertrude began, her voice firm and clear. "I know we're all still reeling from recent events, but it's time we take action to protect ourselves and our neighbors."

She paused, allowing her words to sink in. The room fell silent, all eyes fixed on her.

"Evelyn and I have developed a comprehensive security plan," Gertrude continued, her tone brooking no argument. "First, we're implementing a buddy system for all residents. No one goes out alone, day or night."

Gertrude's gaze swept the room, noting the nods of agreement. She pressed on, her voice gaining strength.

"Second, we're installing new security cameras and improved lighting throughout the community. And third, we're organizing regular self-defense classes tailored for seniors."

As she spoke, Gertrude couldn't help but feel a surge of pride. We're not helpless victims, she thought fiercely. We're survivors, and we're fighting back.

Beside her, Evelyn Davis nodded in agreement, her blonde hair bobbing slightly. Gertrude caught her eye, seeing the same determination reflected there.

"Evelyn, would you like to add anything?" Gertrude asked, stepping aside.

Evelyn approached the microphone, her posture radiating calm authority. "Thank you, Gertrude. I'd like to stress the importance of community vigilance," she said, her voice measured and reassuring. "We're only as strong as our weakest link. Look out for your neighbors, report any suspicious activity, and don't be afraid to ask for help."

As Evelyn spoke, Gertrude observed the audience. Some were furiously scribbling notes, while others nodded along, their faces set with resolve. This is how we heal, Gertrude thought. By taking control, by refusing to be victims.

Mary Simmons carefully arranged the last chair in a perfect circle, her weathered hands smoothing out an invisible wrinkle on the seat. The small community room felt intimate, almost sacred. She glanced at the clock, her heart quickening as the minute hand inched closer to the hour.

The door creaked open, and Mary's gentle brown eyes met those of a hesitant woman entering the room. "Welcome," Mary said softly, her voice warm and inviting. "Please, make yourself comfortable."

As more survivors trickled in, Mary observed each one, noting the tension in their shoulders, the wary glances. She recognized the weight they carried, having borne it herself for so long.

Once everyone was seated, Mary took her place in the circle. She closed her eyes briefly, centering herself. When she opened them, she saw a room full of expectant faces, some etched with fear, others with cautious hope.

"Thank you all for coming," Mary began, her voice low but clear. "I know it wasn't easy to walk through that door today."

She paused, allowing her words to settle. The silence in the room was palpable, thick with unspoken stories and shared pain.

"We're here to support each other," Mary continued, her eyes meeting each person's gaze. "To share our experiences, if we choose, and to find strength in our collective resilience."

A woman to Mary's left shifted in her seat. "How..." she started, her voice barely above a whisper. "How do we even begin?"

Mary nodded, understanding the enormity of the question. "We begin by acknowledging our pain," she said gently. "And by recognizing that we're not alone in it."

As Mary spoke, she felt the room's energy shift. The tension began to ebb, replaced by a tentative sense of solidarity. She watched as shoulders relaxed slightly, as eyes began to meet across the circle.

"Would anyone like to share their story?" Mary asked, her tone conveying that there was no pressure, only invitation.

For a moment, silence reigned. Then, a man cleared his throat. "I... I think I would," he said, his voice trembling but determined.

As he began to speak, Mary felt a wave of emotion wash over her. We're taking the first step, she thought. Together, we're reclaiming our narratives, our lives.

The room listened, rapt with attention and empathy, as the man's story unfolded. Mary knew that this was just the beginning of a long journey, but in this moment, in this circle of survivors, hope had taken root.

The fluorescent lights buzzed overhead as reporters hunched over their desks, the clatter of keyboards a constant backdrop in the newsroom. Editor-in-chief Melissa Chen strode through the bullpen, her sharp gaze sweeping across the room.

"Listen up, people," she called out, her voice cutting through the noise. "We're shifting gears. The Thompson case is old news."

A young reporter, Jake's friend Tom, looked up from his screen. "But the community's still reeling. Shouldn't we—"

"We've milked that story dry," Melissa interrupted. "It's time to move on. I want fresh angles, new leads. What else is happening in this town?"

As the reporters began to pitch ideas, Tom's mind wandered. He thought of Jake, of the toll the case had taken on his friend. The public might be ready to move on, but the scars remained.

Outside, in a small café downtown, two elderly women huddled over steaming mugs of coffee.

"I still check my locks twice before bed," one confessed, her hands trembling slightly.

Her companion nodded. "I know what you mean. But we can't live in fear forever, can we?"

Across the street in the park, a young mother watched her child on the swings, her eyes darting nervously at every passerby.

"It's over," she whispered to herself. "We're safe now." But the tension in her shoulders betrayed her lingering unease.

The town was healing, but slowly. The shadow of Billy Thompson's crimes still loomed large, a reminder of trust betrayed and innocence lost.

The aroma of freshly brewed coffee wafted through the air as Jake slid into the booth across from Samantha. Her fingers drummed an anxious rhythm on the ceramic mug, steam rising in lazy spirals.

"How's it going, Sam?" Jake's voice was low, tinged with concern.

Samantha's eyes met his, a flicker of vulnerability crossing her face. "Nightmares are less frequent now. You?"

Jake ran a hand through his short-cropped hair. "Getting there. Doc says I'm making progress, whatever that means."

A wry smile tugged at Samantha's lips. "Yeah, mine too. As if we can measure healing in neat little checkboxes."

Jake nodded, understanding etched in the lines of his face. "This case... it's changed us, hasn't it?"

"God, yes," Samantha exhaled. "But we're still standing. That's something, right?"

Their eyes locked, a moment of silent camaraderie passing between them. Jake felt a surge of gratitude for his partner, for her unwavering strength.

"We'll get through this, Sam," he said, his voice firm. "One day at a time."

As they parted ways, Jake's mind shifted to his next destination. The drive to Frank Thompson's house was short, but each mile felt heavy with anticipation.

Frank's modest home loomed before him, a physical manifestation of the weight its occupant carried. Jake's knuckles rapped against the door, the sound echoing in the quiet neighborhood.

Frank's face appeared, etched with lines of worry. "Detective Miller," he said, his voice barely above a whisper. "Please, come in."

They settled in the living room, the air thick with unspoken tension. Frank's eyes, filled with a mixture of shame and sorrow, darted around the room, unable to settle on Jake's face.

"I... I can't stop thinking about what Billy did," Frank began, his words stumbling out. "Those poor people... How could my own brother...?"

Jake leaned forward, his posture open but alert. "Frank, your brother's actions aren't your responsibility."

Frank's hands clenched into fists. "Aren't they? I should've seen the signs. I should've done something."

As Frank spoke, Jake's mind raced. How many times had he wrestled with similar thoughts? The weight of hindsight, the burden of 'what-ifs' – they were familiar companions in his line of work.

Jake's eyes softened as he watched Frank struggle with his words. The man's pain was palpable, radiating through the room like a tangible force.

"Frank," Jake said, his voice low and steady. "Guilt can be a heavy burden, especially when it's not ours to carry. I've seen it tear good people apart."

Frank's shoulders slumped. "How do you move on from something like this?"

Jake leaned back, choosing his words carefully. "It's not about moving on. It's about moving forward. Redemption isn't a destination, it's a journey."

"A journey," Frank echoed, his eyes finally meeting Jake's. "I want to make things right, Detective. Not just for those people, but for myself. For my family's name."

Jake nodded, understanding the weight of Frank's words. "That's a noble goal, Frank. It takes courage to face this head-on."

Frank's jaw set, determination flickering in his eyes. "I'm done living in Billy's shadow. I'm going to rebuild what he destroyed, piece by piece if I have to."

"How do you plan to start?" Jake asked, genuinely curious.

"By living with integrity," Frank said, his voice growing stronger. "By being the man I always thought my brother was. I'll volunteer, help the elderly in our community. Show them not all Thompsons are monsters."

Jake felt a surge of respect for the man before him. He offered a reassuring nod, recognizing the sincerity in Frank's words.

"That's a good start, Frank," Jake said. "Remember, you're not alone in this. The community needs people like you now more than ever."

Jake rose from his seat, the floorboards creaking beneath his feet. He extended his hand to Frank, who grasped it firmly.

"Thank you for your time, Frank," Jake said, his voice low and measured. "Your honesty means a lot."

Frank nodded, his eyes glistening. "Just trying to do right, Detective."

Jake stepped out into the crisp evening air, the weight of their conversation settling on his shoulders like a heavy coat. As he walked down the cracked sidewalk, his mind raced.

Justice. Such a simple word, yet so complex in practice. He thought of the victims, their families, even Billy rotting in his cell. The case had left no one untouched.

A car horn blared in the distance, jolting Jake from his reverie. He paused, taking in the quiet neighborhood around him.

"It's not just about punishing the guilty," he muttered to himself. "It's about healing the wounded."

His phone buzzed. A text from Samantha: "How'd it go with Frank?"

Jake typed back: "Better than expected. He's trying to make amends. It's a start."

As he pocketed his phone, Jake's resolve hardened. The case might be closed, but its impact lingered. There was still work to be done.

Across town, in a brightly lit community center, Gertrude leaned over a table covered in blueprints and diagrams. Her blue eyes sparkled with determination as she pointed to a section of the plans.

"We'll need to reinforce these entry points," she said, her voice crisp and authoritative. "No sense in having a security system if the doors themselves are weak."

Evelyn nodded, making a note on her tablet. "Agreed. What about the emergency response protocols?"

Gertrude's lips curled into a small smile. "I've got some ideas about that. Let's run through them one more time."

As they pored over the details, a palpable sense of purpose filled the room. This wasn't just about security measures; it was about reclaiming their sense of safety, their community.

"We're going to make this work, Evelyn," Gertrude said, her tone softening for a moment. "Our people deserve to feel safe in their own homes again."

Evelyn reached out, squeezing Gertrude's hand. "With you leading the charge? I don't doubt it for a second."

They shared a look of understanding before turning back to their work, their resolve unwavering in the face of the challenges ahead.

Chapter 14

Billy Thompson stared at the graffiti-covered wall of his prison cell, the weight of isolation pressing down on him like a physical force. The muffled sounds of inmates in nearby cells only emphasized his solitude. No one spoke to him, no one acknowledged his existence. Even in this den of thieves and murderers, he was an outcast.

He glanced at his cellmate, a burly man with graying hair and hard eyes who hadn't uttered more than a dozen words since Billy arrived. The old-timer's gaze bore into Billy, filled with quiet contempt.

"What're you lookin' at?" Billy snapped, his casual charm evaporating under the pressure.

The cellmate didn't respond, just continued to stare with that same unsettling intensity.

Billy's mind raced. Was this how it would be for the rest of his life? Shunned and despised by even the worst of society? He thought of the elderly victims he'd conned and killed, their trusting faces flashing before his eyes. For the first time, a twinge of regret wormed its way into his chest.

"You know what they're saying about you out there?" the cellmate finally spoke, his voice a low growl.

Billy tensed. "I don't give a damn what they say."

"They say you're worse than scum. That you preyed on the weakest, the most vulnerable."

"It was just business," Billy muttered, but the words sounded hollow even to his own ears.

The cellmate stood, his massive frame casting a shadow over Billy. "There's a code in here, kid. And you? You've broken it."

Billy's heart hammered in his chest. He could feel the cellmate's growing resolve, the shift from disdain to something more dangerous. Justice, prison-style, was coming for William "Billy" Thompson.

The morning bell jolted Billy from his fitful sleep. He blinked, momentarily disoriented, before the harsh reality of his surroundings crashed back into focus. His cellmate was already up, methodically making his bunk with military precision.

"Rise and shine, Billy boy," the older man growled, his voice dripping with sarcasm. "Another beautiful day in paradise."

Billy forced a chuckle, trying to maintain his facade of nonchalance. "Yeah, just another day in the lap of luxury."

As they fell into the familiar routine of morning roll call and breakfast, Billy couldn't shake the feeling of eyes on him. Every inmate they passed seemed to be watching, judging, waiting. He hunched his shoulders, trying to make himself smaller.

"What's the matter, Billy?" his cellmate asked, a dangerous edge to his voice. "Not feeling so chatty today?"

Billy swallowed hard. "Just not a morning person, I guess."

They shuffled through the cafeteria line, the silence between them thick with unspoken tension. Billy's mind raced, trying to figure out how to defuse the situation. He'd always been able to talk his way out of trouble before, but here, his silver tongue seemed to have turned to lead.

"You know," his cellmate said quietly as they sat down, "I've been thinking about what you did. All those old folks, trusting you, and you just..." He trailed off, his fist clenching around his plastic spork.

Billy felt a cold sweat break out on his forehead. "Look, man, it wasn't personal. It was just-"

"Business?" his cellmate finished, his eyes flashing with barely contained rage. "That's what you keep saying. But I'm starting to think you don't understand what that word really means."

As they made their way back to their cell, Billy could feel the noose of justice tightening around his neck. His cellmate's deliberate movements, the way he positioned himself between Billy and the door, it all spoke of a plan coming to fruition.

"After you," the older man said, gesturing for Billy to enter the cell first.

Billy hesitated, his survival instincts screaming at him. But what choice did he have? He stepped inside, his heart pounding so loudly he was sure everyone could hear it.

The cell door clanged shut behind them, and Billy knew, with terrifying certainty, that his time had run out.

The cellmate lunged. A flash of metal. Pain erupted in Billy's side.

"What-" Billy gasped, stumbling backwards.

Another thrust. Sharp. Brutal. The makeshift shiv plunged deep.

Billy's legs gave out. He crumpled to the cold concrete floor, his mind reeling.

"You don't deserve to live," his cellmate hissed, standing over him.

Shock set in. Billy's vision blurred. He pressed his hands to his abdomen, feeling warm blood seep between his fingers.

"I... I didn't..." Billy choked out, his usual smooth talk failing him.

Pain radiated through his body. Each breath was agony. His heart raced, pumping precious life out of him with every beat.

Billy's thoughts scrambled, grasping for understanding. How had it come to this? He'd always been able to talk his way out of trouble, to charm and manipulate. But here, in this cell, his words held no power.

"Please," he whispered, his voice weak and unfamiliar to his own ears.

But there was no mercy in his cellmate's eyes. Only cold, hard justice.

As darkness crept in at the edges of his vision, Billy realized with dawning horror that this was one situation he couldn't scheme his way out of.

As Billy's consciousness wavered, a sudden flood of images washed over him. But instead of the brutal crimes he'd committed, he saw glimpses of a life unlived.

A modest house with a white picket fence materialized. Billy saw himself, clean-shaven and wearing a crisp button-down shirt, mowing the lawn on a sunny Saturday morning.

"Honey, lemonade?" called a faceless woman from the porch.

Billy's lips moved, but no sound came out. He tried to reach for the glass, but his hands remained limp at his sides.

The scene shifted. Now he was seated at a dinner table, surrounded by smiling faces. Children - his children? - laughed as they passed bowls of steaming food.

"Dad, tell us about your day at work," a young boy asked eagerly.

Billy's throat constricted. "I... I don't..." he mumbled, blood bubbling at the corners of his mouth.

Another flash. An office. Billy stood at a podium, receiving an award for years of dedicated service. Applause echoed in his ears, drowning out the harsh reality of his ragged breathing.

"This life," Billy thought desperately, "I could have had this life."

The visions faded, leaving him sprawled on the cold prison floor. The metallic taste of blood filled his mouth. Alarms blared in the distance, a cruel reminder of where he truly was.

"Why?" he croaked, his eyes finding his cellmate's impassive face. "Why didn't I choose differently?"

But there was no answer. Only the stark contrast between the peaceful moments he'd glimpsed and the violent end he'd earned for himself.

As darkness closed in, Billy realized the true cost of his greed. Not just the lives he'd taken, but the life he'd denied himself – a simple, honest existence that now seemed impossibly out of reach.

The cellmate loomed over Billy's crumpled form, his chest heaving with exertion. Sweat beaded on his forehead, mingling with flecks of Billy's blood. His eyes, cold and unforgiving, bore into Billy's fading gaze.

"Justice," the cellmate muttered, his voice barely audible over the din of the prison alarm. He flexed his fingers, still gripping the makeshift shiv. "For all those old folks you preyed on, Thompson."

Billy tried to speak, but only a wet gurgle escaped his lips. His mind raced, desperately clinging to the fading images of the life he'd never have.

The cellmate's lip curled in disgust. "Save your breath, you piece of—"

His words were cut short by the thunderous sound of approaching footsteps. Guards shouted orders, their voices echoing off the concrete walls.

"Cell block D! Multiple officers needed!"

The cellmate's eyes darted to the cell door. He dropped the shiv, letting it clatter to the floor beside Billy.

"What's going on in there?" a guard bellowed, his face appearing in the small window of the cell door.

Billy's vision blurred, the guard's features melting into a hazy smear. He thought of the imaginary children at the dinner table, their laughter now replaced by the cacophony of alarms and shouting.

The cell door burst open, flooding the small space with fluorescent light and the imposing figures of prison guards.

"Holy shit," one guard exclaimed, taking in the bloody scene.

As hands reached for him, Billy's last coherent thought was a bitter realization: his notoriety as the elderly killer had sealed his fate, even among the outcasts of society.

Billy's chest heaved, each shallow breath a struggle. The cold concrete pressed against his cheek, grounding him in his final moments. The cacophony of alarms and shouting faded to a distant hum as his consciousness retreated inward.

"Stay with us, Thompson!" A guard's voice cut through the haze, but Billy was beyond responding.

In his mind's eye, he saw flashes of a mundane life he'd never live. A small house with a white picket fence. A dog wagging its tail. A wife's warm smile.

"I could've..." Billy's thoughts trailed off, his inner voice weak even to himself.

The guard's hands pressed against his wounds, but Billy barely felt the pressure. His body was growing numb, his limbs heavy.

"We're losing him!" someone shouted.

Billy's lips twitched, trying to form words. He wanted to explain, to justify his actions one last time. But no sound came out.

The imaginary life flickered again. A backyard barbecue. Laughing with neighbors. Simple joys he'd traded for greed.

His breath hitched. The cell swam in and out of focus.

With a final, shuddering gasp, Billy's body went limp. The frantic voices and blaring alarms faded to silence, leaving only the echo of a life unlived in the wake of his demise.

The prison intercom crackled to life, its harsh electronic tone cutting through the lingering tension.

"Attention all staff and inmates. Inmate William Thompson, number 24601, has been pronounced dead at 15:47."

The announcement hung in the air, heavy and final. In cells and corridors throughout the prison, a wave of murmurs and whispers arose.

"Good riddance," growled a burly inmate two cells down.

"Guess even scum like him can't escape judgment forever," another voice chimed in.

Guards exchanged glances, their faces a mix of grim satisfaction and weariness. One of them, Officer Martinez, leaned against the wall, shaking his head.

"Never thought I'd see the day," he muttered. "Thompson always acted like he was untouchable."

His partner, Officer Chen, nodded. "Just goes to show, karma catches up to everyone eventually."

Back in the cell, Billy's cellmate sat on his bunk, his face impassive. He stared at the empty space where Billy had fallen, his thoughts hidden behind a stoic mask.

"You reap what you sow," he murmured, more to himself than anyone else.

As the initial shock subsided, a palpable sense of closure settled over the prison. Inmates who had scorned Billy now felt a twisted sort of vindication. Guards who had watched him swagger through his days with unearned confidence now saw justice served in the harshest terms.

The cellmate lay back on his bunk, his actions weighing heavily on his conscience but not enough to overshadow his sense of righteousness. In this brutal world they inhabited, he had become both judge and executioner, meting out the punishment that society's laws had failed to deliver.

As night fell, the prison settled into an uneasy quiet. Billy Thompson's reign of deception and cruelty had come to an abrupt and fitting end, leaving behind a legacy of pain and a stark reminder of the unforgiving nature of life behind bars.

Chapter 15

Jake Miller stood at the window of his cramped office, staring at the gleaming detective's badge in his hand. The weight of the promotion offer hung heavy in the air.

"Sergeant Miller," he muttered, testing how it sounded. All wrong.

His gaze drifted to the wall of unsolved case files. Cold cases that still burned hot in his mind. Faces of victims who deserved justice. He set the badge down with a soft clink.

"Not today," Jake said to the empty room.

He grabbed his jacket and strode out, purpose in every step. The bullpen bustled with activity, but Jake's focus was laser-sharp. Another case waited. Another chance to right a wrong.

His phone buzzed. A text from Sam: "Prepping for elder abuse seminar. Could use your insight on the Hendricks case."

Jake's lips quirked in a half-smile. Sam's dedication matched his own. He fired back a quick reply: "On my way. We'll nail this bastard."

Across town, Samantha Ortiz hunched over a stack of notepads, highlighter in hand. Her dark ponytail swung as she jotted down key points.

"Signs of financial exploitation," she murmured, underlining the phrase. "Unexplained withdrawals, sudden changes in will..."

She paused, a memory flickering. Mrs. Hendricks' bruised arms. The fear in her eyes.

Sam's jaw clenched. "Never again," she vowed, attacking her notes with renewed vigor.

The community needed to know. She'd make damn sure they listened.

Samantha stood at the podium, her eyes scanning the packed auditorium. The hum of anticipation was palpable.

"Elder abuse isn't just physical," she began, her voice steady and clear. "It's financial exploitation, emotional manipulation, neglect."

She clicked to the next slide, a photo of bruised, wrinkled hands filling the screen. A collective gasp rippled through the audience.

"These are the hands of Mrs. Hendricks, 82 years old," Sam continued, her tone laced with controlled anger. "Her own grandson drained her savings, isolated her from family."

Sam's gaze locked with an elderly woman in the front row, tears glistening in the woman's eyes. It fueled her resolve.

"But we can prevent this," Sam urged, leaning forward. "Look for sudden changes in behavior, unexplained injuries, unusual financial activity."

As she spoke, Sam's mind raced. How many Mrs. Hendricks were out there, suffering in silence? Her fists clenched at her sides.

"If you suspect abuse, report it," she emphasized. "You could save a life."

The audience hung on her every word, scribbling notes furiously. Sam felt a surge of hope. This is how change begins, she thought.

Across town, in a cozy café, Gertrude Williams stirred her tea with a mischievous glint in her eye.

"Mary, dear, are you ready to scandalize some youngsters tomorrow?" she asked, her voice carrying a hint of playful defiance.

Mary Simmons chuckled softly, her gentle demeanor a stark contrast to Gertrude's feistiness. "I'm not sure 'scandalize' is the right word, Gert," she replied, her tone warm but firm.

Gertrude waved a hand dismissively. "Potato, po-tah-to. These kids need to know we're not just dusty relics."

Mary nodded, her eyes thoughtful. "It's important they understand the challenges we face," she agreed. "And the wisdom we have to offer."

"Exactly!" Gertrude exclaimed, slapping the table for emphasis. "I say we start with stories from the war. That'll wake them up!"

Mary raised an eyebrow. "Perhaps we should focus on more recent experiences," she suggested gently. "Like navigating healthcare or combating loneliness."

Gertrude's eyes softened. "You're right, as usual," she conceded. "We'll save the war stories for the after-party."

The two friends shared a knowing smile, their bond evident in the comfortable silence that followed.

Gertrude's white hair gleamed under the fluorescent lights as she strode into the high school auditorium, Mary close behind. A sea of young faces turned towards them, curiosity etched on their features.

"Good morning, you little rascals!" Gertrude's voice boomed, her blue eyes twinkling. "Ready to learn from a couple of old broads?"

A ripple of laughter swept through the crowd. Mary stepped forward, her gentle presence a counterpoint to Gertrude's exuberance.

"We're here to talk about respect and protection for the elderly," Mary explained, her soft voice carrying surprising strength. "It's a topic close to our hearts."

Gertrude nodded emphatically. "You bet it is. Now, who here thinks they could take me in a fair fight?"

Several hands shot up, accompanied by good-natured chuckles.

"Think again," Gertrude quipped. "I may look frail, but I've got decades of experience outsmarting whippersnappers like you."

As they continued their presentation, the students leaned forward, captivated. Mary shared stories of isolation and vulnerability, while Gertrude peppered her remarks with sharp wit and hard-earned wisdom.

"Remember," Mary emphasized, her brown eyes scanning the room, "we're not just relics of the past. We're living, breathing individuals with dreams and fears, just like you."

Gertrude chimed in, "And we've got killer dance moves. Don't let anyone tell you different."

The laughter that followed was warm and genuine. Gertrude felt a swell of pride. We're making a difference, she thought. These kids are really listening.

Across town, Frank Thompson sat at his cluttered desk, surrounded by stacks of paperwork. His fingers traced the edge of a form bearing his new name: Frank Thompson, not Franklin Holloway.

"It's the right choice," he muttered to himself, his voice gruff with emotion. "A fresh start."

Frank's eyes fell on a framed photo of smiling seniors at a care facility. His charity's first success story. A sense of purpose washed over him, easing the weight of his past.

"This is how I make amends," he thought, reaching for another grant application. "One life at a time."

Frank Thompson straightened his tie, took a deep breath, and strode into the conference room. Five potential donors sat around the polished oak table, their eyes fixed on him.

"Ladies and gentlemen," Frank began, his deep voice resonating with sincerity, "thank you for being here today."

He laid out his vision for elderly care initiatives, his calloused hands gesturing passionately. "Every dollar we raise is a step towards preventing another tragedy like the one that struck our community."

A woman with silver-streaked hair leaned forward. "Mr. Thompson, your dedication is admirable, but why this cause specifically?"

Frank's jaw tightened. He's gotta be honest. "My brother... he was responsible for those deaths. I can't undo his actions, but I can honor the victims by protecting others."

The room fell silent. Frank's heart pounded. Have I blown it?

"That's... incredibly brave," the woman said softly. Others nodded in agreement.

Relief flooded Frank as he continued his pitch, determination burning in his eyes.

***

Sunlight filtered through the trees in Memorial Park, casting dappled shadows on the gathering crowd. A gentle breeze carried the scent of freshly cut grass and the faint perfume of nearby flowers.

Frank stood at the edge of the crowd, watching as people arrived in small groups. Hushed conversations and quiet sniffles filled the air.

"Never thought I'd see the day," he murmured to himself, scanning the faces – some tear-stained, others stoic. "A community healing, despite what Billy did."

A young woman placed a bouquet at the base of a newly installed memorial plaque. Frank's chest tightened. So many lives changed forever.

As more people filtered in, the atmosphere shifted. There was sorrow, yes, but also a palpable sense of resilience. Frank overheard snippets of conversation:

"Remember how she always baked those incredible pies?"

"He would've loved seeing everyone come together like this."

Frank closed his eyes, allowing the bittersweet memories to wash over him. When he opened them, he saw a future where his work could prevent such gatherings. It won't bring them back, he thought, but it's a start.

Detective Jake Miller arrived at the park, his eyes scanning the crowd with professional instinct. Beside him, Officer Samantha Ortiz adjusted her collar, her posture rigid but her eyes soft with empathy.

"Quite a turnout," Jake murmured, nodding to a fellow officer.

Samantha's gaze swept over the gathered faces. "It's more than just closure, isn't it? It's like... rebirth."

Jake's jaw tightened. "After what this community's been through, they deserve it." His mind flashed to late nights poring over case files, the frustration, the breakthroughs. "We did good, Sam."

"We did," she agreed, a small smile tugging at her lips. "But our work's not done."

Jake spotted a familiar face in the crowd. "There's Chief Ramirez. We should—"

"Jake! Samantha!" a warm voice called out.

They turned to see Gertrude Williams approaching, Mary Simmons at her side. The two elderly women moved with purpose, their eyes bright despite the somber occasion.

"Ladies," Jake greeted, his usually gruff tone softening. "It's good to see you."

Gertrude's blue eyes twinkled. "Wouldn't miss it for the world, dear. Someone's got to keep an eye on you youngsters."

Mary reached out, squeezing Samantha's hand. "Your seminar last week was wonderful. We've already had three people reach out about starting a neighborhood watch."

Samantha beamed. "That's fantastic. Your advocacy work is really making waves."

Jake watched as people gravitated towards Gertrude and Mary, offering hugs and words of gratitude. He leaned in to Samantha. "They've become quite the local celebrities, haven't they?"

Samantha nodded. "And rightfully so. Their resilience... it's inspiring."

As the service was about to begin, Jake felt a mix of emotions wash over him. Pride in their accomplishments, sorrow for the lives lost, and hope for the future. He caught Samantha's eye, seeing the same feelings reflected there.

"Ready?" she asked quietly.

Jake took a deep breath. "As we'll ever be."

Frank Thompson stood at the edge of the gathering, his calloused hands clasped tightly in front of him. The weight of the moment pressed down on his broad shoulders as he scanned the faces in the crowd, a mix of grief and determination etched on each one.

His thoughts drifted unbidden to Billy, his brother's face flashing in his mind. Frank's jaw clenched, guilt and anger warring within him. He shook his head, forcing the image away.

"No," he muttered to himself. "Not today. This isn't about you, Billy."

Frank's eyes settled on the charity banner he'd helped set up earlier. "Elder Care Alliance" it read in bold letters. A small smile tugged at his lips.

"This is about making things right," he thought, straightening his posture. "One step at a time."

The crowd hushed as Mayor Langley approached the podium, her silver hair catching the late afternoon sun. Frank moved closer, joining the attentive audience.

"Today," the Mayor began, her voice strong despite the emotion evident in her eyes, "we gather not just to mourn, but to honor. To remember those whose lives were cut short, and to celebrate the strength of our community."

Frank felt a lump form in his throat as she continued.

"Each victim was more than just a name. They were our neighbors, our friends, our family. Sarah Johnson, who always had a kind word for everyone she met. Robert Chen, whose garden was the envy of the block..."

As the Mayor spoke, Frank noticed tissues being passed through the crowd. Sniffles and quiet sobs punctuated the air.

"But look around you," Mayor Langley said, her voice rising. "See how we've come together. How we've refused to let darkness win. This tragedy has shown us the true heart of our community."

Frank's gaze swept over the gathered faces, recognizing the determination in their eyes. He caught sight of Detective Miller and ADA Ortiz, standing tall despite the weight they'd carried throughout the investigation.

"We will never forget," the Mayor concluded, her voice thick with emotion. "But we will move forward, stronger and more united than ever before."

As applause rippled through the crowd, Frank felt a renewed sense of purpose. He may not be able to change the past, but he could damn well work to make the future brighter.

"For all of them," he whispered, his resolve hardening. "And for those who need us now."

A hush fell over the crowd as volunteers moved forward, each carrying a white balloon. Jake Miller watched, his jaw tight, as the first balloon was released into the sky.

"For Sarah," someone murmured.

Another balloon followed. "For Robert."

One by one, the balloons ascended, each carrying a name, a memory, a life cut short. Jake felt Samantha's hand on his arm, squeezing gently. He glanced at her, seeing his own mix of emotions reflected in her eyes.

"We did it, Sam," he said softly. "We got justice for them."

She nodded, her voice barely above a whisper. "But at what cost?"

As the last balloon drifted upward, Jake's gaze was drawn to Gertrude and Mary. The two women stood hand in hand, their faces etched with a complex blend of sorrow and hope.

"Ladies," Jake said, approaching them. "How are you holding up?"

Gertrude's piercing blue eyes met his. "We're still here, Detective. That's something, isn't it?"

Mary nodded, her gentle voice carrying a note of steel. "And we'll keep fighting. For all of us who can't."

Jake felt a surge of admiration for their resilience. He was about to respond when he noticed Frank Thompson join their small group.

"I hope I'm not intruding," Frank said, his expression cautious but determined.

"Not at all," Samantha replied, her tone warm. "I think we all belong here together."

As they stood in silence, watching the last of the balloons disappear into the azure sky, Jake felt a shift in the air. It wasn't just the end of a case or a memorial service. It was the beginning of something new.

"You know," he said, looking at each face in turn, "I think we've all been changed by this. But maybe... maybe that's not such a bad thing."

Gertrude's wry chuckle broke the solemnity. "Well, Detective, I'd say that's the understatement of the year."

Their laughter, soft but genuine, mingled with the gentle breeze. As Jake looked at these people - survivors, advocates, fellow seekers of justice - he realized they'd forged a bond that went beyond the boundaries of a typical case.

"So," he said, a hint of a smile on his face, "what's next for all of us?"

The sun began its descent, painting the sky in a palette of warm oranges and deep purples. Jake's gaze swept over the gathered crowd, their faces softened by the golden hour light.

"What's next?" Mary echoed, her gentle voice carrying a hint of wonder. "I suppose we keep living, keep remembering."

Gertrude nodded, her blue eyes sharp as ever. "And we keep fighting for those who can't fight for themselves."

Jake felt a surge of purpose course through him. "You're right," he said, his voice low but firm. "This isn't the end. It's a new beginning."

As he spoke, he noticed people starting to disperse, their conversations a low murmur carried on the evening breeze. Families embraced, friends clasped hands, strangers exchanged nods of understanding.

"Look at them," Samantha whispered, her eyes glistening. "They're healing, right before our eyes."

Jake watched as an elderly couple, arms linked, made their way slowly down the park path. A group of teenagers helped a frail woman to her feet, their faces etched with kindness.

"It's beautiful," Frank murmured, his voice thick with emotion. "This is why we do what we do."

As the sun dipped lower, casting long shadows across the grass, Jake felt a profound sense of peace settle over him. The case had been brutal, the losses devastating, but here, in this moment, he saw hope.

"We've all been through hell," he said, looking at each of his companions in turn. "But we're still standing. And we're not alone."

The warm glow of sunset bathed their faces, a physical manifestation of the warmth Jake felt in his chest. As darkness began to creep in around the edges of the park, he knew with certainty that this community would continue to heal, to grow stronger.

And he would be there, every step of the way.

Don't miss out!

Visit the website below and you can sign up to receive emails whenever Shane Reed publishes a new book. There's no charge and no obligation.

https://books2read.com/r/B-A-LSDAB-TOBMF

BOOKS 2 READ

Connecting independent readers to independent writers.

Did you love *The Last Breath*? Then you should read *Shadows of a Perfect Life*[1] by Shane Reed!

[2]

In the pursuit of perfection, Robert has clawed his way to the top, crafting an enviable life that hides a chilling secret. But beneath the polished exterior lies a simmering resentment—a festering wound inflicted by a mother whose expectations seem insatiable. As the pressure mounts and the façade begins to crack, Robert's desperation leads him down a dark path.

When he makes the unthinkable decision to hire a hitman to silence the voice that has haunted him for years, Robert finds himself entangled in a web of deceit and bloodshed. The plan spirals out of control, and a bloody handprint becomes the key piece of evidence that threatens to unravel everything he has built.

---

1. https://books2read.com/u/b6qxDE

2. https://books2read.com/u/b6qxDE

As the police close in and the stakes grow higher, Robert must confront not only the consequences of his actions but also the ghosts of his past. Will he find redemption, or will his dark choices consume him?

In "Shadows of a Perfect Life," explore the depths of human nature and the haunting repercussions of unchecked ambition. This gripping tale of betrayal and moral decay will keep you on the edge of your seat until the very last page.

Also by Shane Reed

A Conning Couple Novel
Checkmate
The Great Escape
The Queen's Gambit
The Sicilian Defense
Fool's Mate
The Scottish Game
Stale Mate
The Conning Couple Books 1-5

True Crime
The Sniffing Dog Scam
The Vengeful Parent
The Psychic Scam
Conterfeit Capitalist
Innocence On Trial
The Deceptive Dream
Voices Of Deception
Shadows of a Perfect Life
Unjust Conviction
Clown Killer
Redemption

The Last Breath

www.ingramcontent.com/pod-product-compliance
Lightning Source LLC
Chambersburg PA
CBHW020557160726
47991CB00002B/760